Chambers desperately tried to level out the plane. If he could make the 747 hit the water belly-first, instead of nose-first, they might all have some chance of survival. He tried to lower the flaps and thereby slow down their airspeed, but by this time most of the plane's systems were no longer functional. The plane bucked and reared as it went down. Desperately Chambers continued to pull back on the wheel with all his strength. He had almost leveled out the 747 when the plane's belly hit the water with tremendous force. The shock was like being caught in the middle of a tremendous explosion.

Steve's scream was buried amid the welter of sounds that seemed to swell up like a geyser—the tearing and twisting of metal, the sounds of human fear and pain.

The plane shuddered and rolled toward one side. Gallagher grabbed a partition to steady himself and, to his horror, saw a guest rushing toward the tottering wall-size television. The television unit teetered, then, in an avalanche of metal and broken glass, fell, striking the guest on the head, then pinning him to the floor.

Then, just as suddenly as it had happened, the force of initial impact was over.

AIRPORT '77

A novel by Michael Scheff and David Spector
based upon their screenplay

Inspired by the novel AIRPORT
by Arthur Hailey

A BERKLEY MEDALLION BOOK
published by
BERKLEY PUBLISHING CORPORATION

1

Philip Stevens pushed forward on the stick of the small Bell helicopter. It swooped in an arc through the cloudless blue Florida sky. Suddenly, far below, the restless Atlantic Ocean was replaced by a narrow finger of land covered by lush green lawns, palm trees, and a canallike network of roadways.

A broad grin crossed Stevens' face. Even from this height the landscape was unmistakable and familiar. They were over that fabulous stretch of land called Palm Beach. Stevens turned to his copilot and signaled him to take over the controls. The copilot nodded, took the stick, and continued edging the copter down toward the land below.

Philip Stevens had handed over the controls so he could better enjoy the view. Although he had lived in Palm Beach for most of his life, he never tired of it, never lost the thrill of the first time he had seen that seemingly unending chain of mansions and cool green lawns. Stevens moved in his seat and tried to find a comfortable position. He stretched out his lanky frame as best he could in the helicopter's cramped surroundings. He was well over six feet, and although he was nearing seventy, there was no stoop in his frame. Philip Stevens' age was easily forgotten. Although his hair was streaked with gray, and his face was carved by lines, what drew people to Philip Stevens were his eyes. They were blue, piercing, and still curious about the world around him. They were the eyes of a man who in his old age still retained the intensity of his youth. He was one of those men whom time seems not to wear down, but to strip of all superfluities, so that what remained was a hard kernel of character.

He zipped down the top of his sheepskin windbreaker and felt the coolness of the air blowing through the copter's bubble. He breathed deeply of its freshness and felt somewhat revived. He had just spent the past day and night with angry labor negotiators in an overheated room thick with the odor of too many cigars and cigarettes. He glanced at his watch. He had been in there literally twenty-four hours.

It had been worth it, though. In the forty-five years since he had founded it, Stevens Corporation had never suffered a plant shutdown due to labor trouble. Through his efforts, that possibility had been averted again.

When he received word that, with twelve hours to go before expiration of the old contract, negotiations at the Jacksonville textile plant had stalemated, Philip Stevens had acted immediately. By three A.M. he had boarded a plane out of New York, heading toward Jacksonville.

He then personally commanded the negotiating team for the plant. It had been a physical-endurance test that stretched from midmorning through the afternoon and then into the steamy Florida night. He played an old game, but one that was both exciting and fulfilling. Alternately tough and jocular, Stevens impressed the union leaders with his courage and his obvious desire to make a compromise that was fair to both sides. Shortly after dawn, agreement had been reached. Amid the smell of sweat, smoke, and anxiety, the new contract was signed.

Remembering the long night, Stevens felt a thrill of exhilaration ripple through his body. The give-and-take of negotiation, the suspense of the impending deadline. It had all brought back memories of the early days, when he was founding the corporation that now bore his name.

"Well," he thought, "I'll be gone soon enough. I've got a team that can carry on after I'm gone, and do a damn fine job. But while I'm here, I'm sure going to let people know that I've got some life in me yet."

Stevens smiled. Everyone kept telling him to slow down—the members of the board, his friends, his family. Still, they'd just have to understand that to an old warhorse the sound of the battle horns would always be an overpowering attraction.

As the helicopter lost altitude, the details of Palm Beach became clearer. The huge Spanish-style mansions, with their thick stucco walls and red-tile roofs, lost their diminutive toylike appearance and began to take on the solidity and detail that was unique to these magnificent homes.

The copter pilot dropped lower as he made his way toward the west end of the peninsula, where Stevens' estate was located. Smiling, Stevens breathed in the wonderful briny air off the ocean. His eyes misted over for a moment as he caught sight of his estate. Of all the places he had lived in his long life—and there had been many—this was the place he had come to call home.

The estate had been built in the middle twenties. Its first owners had called it Milleflora, place of a thousand flowers. After purchasing the estate, Stevens had done his best to make that name literally true. The huge mansion was flanked by acre upon acre of carefully cultivated gardens. The estate was so large, it contained over a mile of roadways. To the south there was a small artificial lake that was well stocked with fish. Stevens had personally supervised its construction. To the north, an arboretum that contained rare plants from the four corners of the world.

But Stevens' pride and joy was at the center of the estate, and now, as it came into view, Stevens felt a warm surge through his body.

It was known, quite simply, as the mansion. Spanish in architectural design, it was four stories high. Balconies ran the entire length of the outside, and the intense purple of bourgainvillea climbed the sides of the building to reach them. It was like something out of a fairy tale.

The copilot pushed forward on the stick, and the helicopter began its noisy descent toward the lawn. The

3

long driveway was jammed with trucks, and uniformed workmen were lifting crates from the trucks onto the lawn. Other workmen carefully dollied the crates to their destination—the large oaken doors, now thrown wide, that led into the mansion. Television trucks had already arrived, and thick electrical cables snaked over the lawn and driveway. The constant stream of workmen reminded Stevens of an ant colony.

The copter settled onto the lawn, and its rotor blades slowed. Stevens took off his windbreaker. Already the day was beginning to heat up, and it was only a little past ten. Stevens could see Harry Jefferson and his men as they came down the long curved stone steps that led to the mansion's entrance and hurried toward the copter. He noted that Harry was wearing a suit, even in this heat. Harry had been with Stevens, and the corporation, from just about the beginning. He was an invaluable public-relations man, and if anybody could keep calm and order amidst this chaos, it was Harry.

Stevens stepped out of the plane and was immediately surrounded by reporters. They elbowed each other as they took pictures of him. He thought that after being in the public eye for over fifty years, people must be tired of seeing his picture in magazines and newspapers. Stevens grinned at the reporters and held up his arms.

"Hell, boys, don't waste that film on me. Save it for the opening tonight. It's going to be quite a wing-ding. Or so they tell me."

A barrage of questions flew through the air. With all the reporters shouting to be heard, it sounded like the scramble of noise you get on a radio that hasn't been tuned properly. But it didn't matter to Stevens whether he heard the questions or not, because he knew exactly what they were going to ask. They were the same questions that he had been asked over the past year, ever since it had been announced that Philip Stevens was turning over his Florida estate to the people of the United States. Still, the reporters were there to ask questions, and Stevens was there to answer them. Good-naturedly, he began to tell

4

about his plan for what seemed, to him, the thousandth time. He told how, approaching seventy, he had felt foolish, living alone on the huge estate. How he felt he owed a debt to America and to the American people. For where else could he, a young man off the farm, become, through the sweat of his brow, the owner of one of the world's largest corporations. So, out of this had emerged his plan. He decided to turn the mansion into a gallery to hang his extensive collection of art. The enormous grounds would be turned into a park, and the whole kit and caboodle, worth millions, would be turned over to the people of the United States.

Harry Jefferson broke into the circle of reporters.

"Later, boys, later," he said. "Mr. Stevens has just arrived, we've got a thousand things to do to make sure this opening happens tonight. No opening, no news story—right, boys?"

The reporters laughed. They had been smoothly and diplomatically told to brush off.

"We've set out some refreshments for you over in the garden house. It looks like it's getting hot, and I'm sure you gentlemen are thirsty. By the way, we've prepared some press kits for you, and you'll find them next to the bourbon."

That got another laugh out of the reporters, and after promising them a press conference later in the day, Jefferson guided Stevens away from them and toward the steps of the mansion. Jefferson extracted a cigar from his coat pocket and lit it as he and Stevens made their way through the workmen and trucks to the mansion.

As they mounted the steps to the huge hand-carved oak doors, Stevens' eyes were caught by the intense purple of the bougainvillea. He remembered planting it the day he purchased the estate. Those scraggly little plants now had grown to wrap the mansion all the way to the roof. He supposed that over the years he had watched it climb and grow, but the period of time was so long that the plants' growth had been invisible to him. It was not unlike the experience of watching his only child, Lisa, grow up.

From a baby she suddenly seemed to spring into a gawky adolescence. Then, just as suddenly, she was a beautiful young woman. And then, even more quickly, or so it seemed, she was married.

Inside, in what had been the living room of the mansion, there was a flurry of activity. This room had been converted into the main gallery of Stevens' new art museum. Paintings were being hung, spotlights adjusted, floors polished. After months of preparation, the museum was just about ready to open.

Stevens looked around him. The cool white of the room provided the perfect setting for the paintings and sculptures that were being put into place. It was clear that the eclectic mixture of art in the room reflected an impeccable taste. Stevens was a collector who had always known what he liked and had had the unlimited funds necessary to implement those tastes.

Fascinated, Stevens watched as workmen carefully completed the hanging of a large Calder mobile. In place, it provided a focus for the large room. Stevens was more than pleased. As he watched the mobile slowly move and turn, he thought that it looked as if it had been created to hang only in this room. Suddenly, his concentration was interrupted by a voice.

"Mr. Stevens, could I ask you a few questions?"

Stevens turned and saw that the voice belonged to Marcie Thompson, a pert blonde who worked as a news reporter for a Miami TV station. Before he could answer, Jefferson spoke up.

"I thought I shooed all you reporters out to the garden," he said.

"You know I don't like bourbon, Harry," she replied with a smile. That brought a laugh from both Stevens and Jefferson. They liked the young reporter, and she was shrewd enough to press the advantage while they were still laughing. She began a barrage of rapid-fire questions. With a sigh, Stevens began the familiar routine. But Marcie felt that there was a slant on a different sort of story, one that Stevens could help her cover. Marcie wanted to do a story about Philip Stevens' corporate jet that would be bringing a group of Stevens' friends and business associates to tonight's museum opening. With a twinkle in his eye, Stevens shrugged.

"It's just a new company plane. My friends are gathered in Washington, D.C., for the flight down here. There's nothing special about that."

Marcie knew that Stevens was kidding her. She reacted with mock exasperation.

"Nothing special about a 747 that cost you twenty-five million dollars to buy, then another fifteen million dollars to refurbish? Come on, Mr. Stevens, what kind of reporter do you take me for?"

Stevens turned to Harry Jefferson. "I see this young woman's done her homework." He turned to Marcie again.

"How'd you get that information? We never released the cost figures on that 747."

Marcie smiled. "I kept calling around at Boeing until I found someone who felt like chatting."

"Not bad," Stevens replied. "That's very enterprising."

"I understand that the plane's been overhauled. The passenger seats have been taken out, and you've built offices and conference rooms aboard."

"And much more than that," Stevens replied. "I'll tell you what. Join me at the Palm Beach airport tonight. Bring along your news-film crew. I'll take you on a personal tour of the plane."

Marcie filled with enthusiasm. Impulsively she gave Stevens a hug. "That's great. If you do that, the network might even pick it up as a news feature."

"Good. I hope they do," Stevens said.

Smiling, Stevens watched as Marcie hurried away, in search of her newsreel crew.

Jefferson turned to him. "She's full of piss and vinegar, that one. We'll be seeing her on the network someday."

"I don't doubt it for a minute," Stevens smiled.

But as Marcie strode away, Stevens' spirit seemed to visibly sag. It was as if her energy and youthful

7

enthusiasm reminded him of some nagging problem. He turned to Jefferson.

"Has Eve Clayton called yet?"

"We've been trying to reach her, but she's between the Washington office and Dulles."

Tensely Stevens nodded. "I see. Let me know the minute you get hold of her."

"Of course. Phil, is there something I can do?"

Stevens turned to him with a sad smile. He put his arm around Jefferson's shoulder.

"No, old friend. It's a personal problem. And I'm afraid it's all in Eve Clayton's hands now."

Jefferson returned Stevens' warm smile. He had been in Stevens' inner circle of friends for so many years that he knew whatever was bothering Stevens must be of critical importance, otherwise Stevens would have certainly confided in him.

2

Callahan's teeth hurt.

He'd been conscious of the ache since early afternoon. And now, as he drove through the outskirts of Roanoke, he wondered if he'd forgotten his yearly appointment with the dentist. He was not a methodical or an orderly man. Consequently, he couldn't remember whether or not he'd recently received one of those little cards that Dr. Sloan sent out to remind him to make an appointment. But he did know that his teeth hurt—oh, yes indeed, that he knew.

He checked his watch, then downshifted his shabby Plymouth and turned the corner onto Oak Street. It was almost noon, and traffic was steadily increasing. He felt a flutter of panic. What if he got there late? Would they wait for him? Suddenly a progression of fearful thoughts flooded him. What if they didn't show up? How would he put it back? It had been hard enough to get it out of there—but to put it back! The until now unregarded possibility filled him with raw fear.

Callahan sped up, then jammed on the brakes, narrowly missing a new Cadillac that had stopped for a pedestrian ahead of him. He squinted into the afternoon sun and noted the occupant of the Cadillac. "Rich son of a bitch," he thought. Until the light changed and the car moved away, Callahan continued to regard the Cadillac with a bitterness he reserved for all those who seemed to have more than he.

He slid the gearshift into first, turned off Fourth Street, and made his way down Thompson. Traffic was much lighter on this side street, and he knew he'd have no problem getting to his destination on time. He lit a cigarette and tried to relax, but the ache in his jaw persisted.

Callahan wrinkled his nose in disgust as he passed the rows of sagging wooden apartment buildings. The buildings were relics of wartime. They had been put up quickly, designed to meet the housing needs of the hundreds of workers who flocked to Roanoke to work in the shipyards and at the military bases. Thirty-five years later, they were still standing, occupied now mostly by blacks and Puerto Ricans. Callahan was slowed as a bus stopped and disgorged its load of people returning from work. Children played in the streets, and here and there groups of black men sat on stoops, drinking beers in the last minutes of fading autumn sunlight. Callahan shook his head. Even when he was a kid, Roanoke hadn't been much of a city. Now it was nothing but a goddamned slum.

Callahan thought nervously about the green cylinder that rested in the trunk of the car. It was well wrapped in blankets, so he knew it was safe from harm. Still, although he didn't know what the cylinder contained, he would feel a lot safer when he had turned it over to the men who had hired him.

A little ahead of schedule, he carefully drove through the fringes of the city's tenderloin district. The garish neon of the taverns he passed seemed to beckon. He was convinced that a quick shot of gin would take care of the ache he felt in his jaw. He glanced at his watch. He'd picked up seven minutes by using this side street. Still, he didn't dare risk being late. He thought about the thousand dollars they had promised him. It was some consolation—but he wished he could have a drink.

He reached the corner of Third and Lake three minutes ahead of schedule, pulled to the curb, and parked in front of an out-of-business restaurant. He turned off the engine and settled down to wait. Suddenly a moment of raw panic as a police cruiser slowed, eyeballed him, then sped up again as it passed. Operating from an impatient desire to do something, as much as from a recollection that he had been instructed to create a cover, he quickly got out of the car, strolled to the corner, and purchased the evening paper from a coin-operated machine. When he returned to his car, the white van was already there, parked behind him. His heart began to pound as he approached the men who had hired him to steal the small green cylinder that now rested in his trunk.

As he moved to join the men, he finally realized that his teeth hurt because he had been clenching them for the past three hours.

"Dulles Tower, this is Two Three Sierra, Heavy. We're out of three thousand IFR for landing."

"Roger, Two Three Sierra. Continue approach. Cleared for landing."

Flight Captain Don Gallagher switched the 747 out of autopilot and began losing altitude. Deftly he coordinated the plane's descent with a decrease in the thrust of the jet engines. The sustained roar of the engines quieted as the big plane slowed. Gallagher handled the plane with long-practiced ease. As the plane entered the flight pattern for Dulles airport, his eyes flicked from instrument to instrument, noting fuel flow here, rate of deceleration there, radio altimeter setting, directly in front of him. He was a man in his early forties, although his salt-and-pepper hair and mustache led people to believe he was much older. He was small, wiry, and with an almost unflappable calm that made him entirely reliable as the captain of this huge plane. Gallagher turned to his copilot, Robert Chambers.

"She's all yours."

Chambers nodded and took over the controls. Gallagher turned and spoke to the flight engineer, Les Walker.

"Did you get the landing data?"

"It's prepared. The pressurization's set," Walker replied.

"No bugs?"

Walker shook his head. This was the final checkout flight, and everything had been adjusted and tuned perfectly.

"Clean as a whistle."

Gallagher smiled and settled into his seat. It had been a good test flight. Which was to say that, after many such flights, the new plane had checked out A-1 perfect. It had been a rigorous series of tests, checking and rechecking the handling of the big plane, methodically running through the functions of each of the six backup systems that made the 747 the safest airplane flying.

Gallagher glanced out the side window. As the plane descended, the cloud cover over Washington was breaking up. He could see intermittent flashes of the ground below—flashes that came and went so fast between the ends of obscuring clouds that the sight had the quality of the flickering of a silent movie. The bad visibility hardly mattered. They were landing on instruments. Anyway, Gallagher had guided 747s through the landing pattern into Dulles airport so many times that he could have landed with the autopilot off, and blindfolded, if he had to.

Walker picked up the checklist and began to go through the descent and pre-landing checks. Each time a 747 landed, the crew, as a normal operating procedure, checked and set the systems used during the descent and landing. Walker read aloud the items on the checklist, and Gallagher and Chambers answered after checking each item on their control panel.

"Pressurization?"

"Set."

"Altimeters?"

"Reset and cross-checked."

"Airspeed and EPR bugs?"

"Set."

"Baro set unit?"

"Reset and cross-checked."

The familiar litany went on and on. There were more

12

than one hundred items that had to be checked off the list before the 747 landed.

The plane continued its descent. The clouds pulled away, and there, miles ahead of them, in the clear, was Dulles. Gallagher glanced, for a moment, out of the side window to the south. High above were fluffy cumulus clouds, bounded by grayer and darker clouds that faded off into the horizon. The profound contrast of the clouds was attractive to the eye. But as an experienced pilot, Gallagher knew that the cloud formation indicated there would be bad weather for several days, extending down the Atlantic seacoast. He hoped that Philip Stevens hadn't planned any outdoor activities for the museum opening tonight. The weather reports said there was a good chance of storms in Florida.

Gallagher watched as Chambers went through the landing routine. On this test flight, Gallagher was making it his business to check out his crew as well as the aircraft. Gallagher watched Chambers trim the engines, then set the flaps for their final descent. He noticed the precision of Chambers' timing. There was no question but that the man knew what he was doing.

Gallagher's headset crackled.

"Two Three Sierra. You are cleared for final approach."

Gallagher clicked on his microphone. "Roger, Dulles Tower. Out."

He nodded to Chambers, and the copilot began to bring the large craft down toward the blinking beacon that marked the end of the Dulles runway. In the distance, Gallagher could see the ultramodern tower and arrivals building.

Gallagher watched as they made their landing approach. He joined the men in the intricate routine of landing, but continued to wonder about Chambers. Something about the man didn't sit right with him.

As a general rule, Gallagher liked to know his flight crew well. He had worked with Walker before, and knew him as a conscientious flight engineer. Walker had a lightning-quick sense of humor and an easygoing nature. When you considered the cramped space of the 747's cockpit, and the long hours that the three crew members had to spend together, then that trait of Walker's became a very desirable quality. Also, and most important, Walker was good, damned good.

But Chambers was still a mystery to Gallagher. Although he had been brought on to the project a month after Gallagher, which was to say at the very start, Gallagher could not say he knew the man any better now than then. Chambers was a physically large man, in his early forties. But he seemed to tend toward a humorlessness. Gallagher would always laugh at Walker's jokes, but Chambers never would. It wasn't that Walker's humor irritated him. He seemed to patiently tolerate them. That, in fact, was the word that Gallagher thought most described Chambers. The word was "tolerate." Chambers never seemed to emotionally react to anything; he very quietly tolerated it. From their months together on the project, Gallagher hadn't even a clue to Chambers' inner life.

Still, the man was good. He knew his job, which from Gallagher was not small praise. It was just that Gallagher wanted to know what made his crew tick. This was not idle curiosity. The more you knew about a crew member—his weak points and his strong points—the more you knew about how that crew member would react in a crisis. In Gallagher's profession, such reactions could mean the difference between life and death. With modern aviation's impressive safety record, with all the automatic instruments they possessed, still it was often a man's judgment that made the difference in an emergency situation.

The 747 cleared the boundaries that marked the Dulles runway. It drew closer to the ground, seemed to hover there for a moment; then, with a small bump, the wheels touched ground and they were once again earthbound.

Hank Buchek stood by the large open doors of Hangar

C, and watched Stevens' 747 land. When it began its taxi toward the hangar, he let out an almost audible sigh of relief.

Earlier in the day Don Gallagher had jokingly assessed Buchek's emotional state as "deteriorating." Unfortunately, Buchek reflected, he had to agree with Gallagher. He *was* a little nervous. By nine-thirty that morning he had already smoked half a pack of cigarettes before he remembered he had quit smoking the day before.

Buchek's nervousness was understandable, though. He was a tense, wiry man known for his explosive temper and his mania for perfection. As supervisor of the Stevens 747 project, he had expended his not inconsiderable energies for over a year and a half on the airplane that Gallagher was now testing.

Buchek leaned against the hangar wall and forced himself to breathe deeply in the damp air. It was the first moment of relaxation he'd had since very early morning. Suddenly the sky, even with the imminence of rain, looked beautiful to him.

This was the day that would culminate all his efforts.

Behind this moment was a year and a half of hard-driving experiment and work that had now narrowed down to an eight-hour deadline. Eight hours for the final preparation, then the loading of the plane, and finally the inaugural flight, this evening, to Palm Beach. And then the 747 would be, at last, out of Buchek's hands.

Although he had enjoyed the 747 project, it had occupied all of his thoughts for too long. It was time he tackled something new.

When he was first presented the 747 job, he had felt highly flattered. Very few of the big planes had been converted from passenger service to private use. It was a great honor to be considered for a job that would involve almost the complete redesign of an existing aircraft. He met with the architects, engineers, builders. It would be his job to turn their ideas into reality. Well, he had achieved that. With generous infusions of Mr. Stevens' money, he and his crews had torn out seating, moved bulkheads, created private compartments, conference rooms, a gourmet kitchen, pressurized cargo holds. In short, he had taken the world's most advanced passenger aircraft and turned it into the world's most luxurious corporate aircraft. Buchek wondered what Stevens' reaction to the finished plane would be. But, underneath, Buchek knew that Stevens would find the plane to be perfection, just as he did.

A small towmotor vehicle, its engine roaring, barreled from inside the hangar and passed Buchek, headed toward the 747, which now loomed closer to the hangar. The small vehicle was the size of a large slab of concrete, painted bright yellow. It was little more than an enormous diesel engine with a cover and wheels, raw power that was hooked onto the wheels of the 747 and then used to slowly haul it to or from the hangar.

Buchek looked up, taking in the full view of the plane as it came to rest a hundred yards from the hangar. Turned slightly away, the bold red of the gigantic S and the logo below it for the Stevens Corporation stood out on the huge tail beneath the morning sun. As the towmotor approached, the high-pitched scream of the plane's jet engines faded. The ground crew was already wheeling a boarding ramp to the plane so that the crew could disembark before the 747 was towed into the hangar. The men and the boarding ramp were dwarfed by the huge size of the plane.

But, Buchek thought, just about everything was dwarfed by the 747. He had been involved with 747s since they first went into production. He still marveled at the unique combination of size and pinpoint technology that comprised them. Tall as a four-story building and half as long as a football field. The plane generated millions of horsepower. In fact, the plane generated enough power to heat and light a medium-sized town for twenty-four hours or more. And yet, combined with all that power was a series of safety backup systems that enabled the 747 to maintain the best safety record in the history of aviation.

Buchek pressed the button on his digital watch. The

16

crimson numbers flashed ten-twenty at him. He took the urgent flashing as almost a personal rebuke. There was still much to do before the plane was scheduled to leave on its maiden flight to Palm Beach. He knew that inside the vast cavern of the 747's hangar, his handpicked maintenance crew was preparing for one more check of the plane. At that moment a small army of mechanics was checking tools, preparing to scurry over the plane when it was tugged into the hangar and moored in place. It would be the final check, but possibly the most thorough. "Well, time to get to work," Buchek thought. He headed toward the approaching 747. He knew that somehow he'd see that everything was done and that the 747 got into the air by six o'clock that night. "So many more things to do, and so little time to do them in," he reflected. He was already exhausted and knew that he would be still more exhausted before the long day was finished. "Well," he thought, "I wanted to be in charge of this damn project, and I got what I wanted."

In the cockpit of the 747, Walker clicked off switches, one by one. They were, at last, nearing the end of the postflight checklist. Walker quickly read through the last few items, then checked them off as Gallagher and Chambers responded.

"Emergency lights?"

"Off."

"Beacon lights?"

"Off."

"Radios?"

"Off," Chambers said, and leaned back in his seat.

Gallagher smiled. "Fine," he said. He turned around in his seat to the flight engineer, Walker. Walker handed him the clipboarded sheets of paper that summarized the results of the checkout flight. Gallagher took a look at them. Things were fine, just as he had expected. He initialed the papers and handed the clipboard back to Walker.

"Okay, gents, she's in good shape for tonight."

Gallagher unbuckled himself from his seat and rose, putting on his blue flight jacket. "Chambers . . . Walker, see you around five o'clock?"

"Sure, Captain," Chambers said.

Walker looked up from stowing his gear into his flight bag.

"Sorry I was late with those boost pumps, Don."

"Don't worry about it. See you fellows later."

Gallagher left the cockpit, closing the door behind him.

Chambers zipped his flight bag closed, then stood up. When he spoke, it surprised Walker, because he couldn't remember Chambers ever having spoken to him when it didn't relate specifically to flight procedure.

"Why even mention the boost pumps? He didn't notice."

It wasn't really a question, and it annoyed Walker.

"He noticed," Walker said.

Chambers smiled. "You're pretty sure."

As Chambers crossed to the door, Walker looked up at him, almost angry now. "Why the hell do you think Stevens hires a guy like Gallagher? He notices everything."

Chambers shrugged as he opened the door to go. With that same annoying half-smile he said, "See you at five, Mr. Walker."

Gallagher came out of the 747 and strode down the boarding ramp, shouldering his flight bag as he walked. He smiled wryly as he saw that Buchek was waiting for him at the foot of the ramp. Buchek looked nervous, as usual, but was trying to maintain an air of nonchalance. Gallagher had known him for fifteen years and knew that to Buchek there was no anxiety like the anxiety of a project supervisor waiting to hear a pilot's final report on an aircraft.

"Well?"

Gallagher smiled. "Relax, Hank. It couldn't have been better. She's perfection."

Buchek visibly seemed to relax. He shrugged. "Of course she is. I wasn't worried at all." He reached into his pocket, extracted a cigarette, then began looking for a match.

Gallagher smiled. "You're not going to light that thing, are you?"

Startled, Buchek took the cigarette out of his mouth and crumpled it into his pocket. "Hell no, I quit."

The two men started walking to the hangar. Behind them, the towmotor coupled to the wheels of the 747 and began towing the plane toward the gaping hangar doors.

Gallagher clapped Buchek on the back. "Well, Hank, now that Stevens has his dream machine, you can get a little rest—go back to that good executive life. Two-hour lunches, golf every Friday..."

Buchek laughed out loud at his friend's description of his supposed daily routine. Unfortunately, Buchek's work on this project wouldn't be finished until after he delivered the 747 to Mr. Stevens in Palm Beach that night. That made Buchek think of the dwindling hours and of all that still remained to be done. "Jesus Christ," he thought, "I've really got to get a move on."

3

Throngs of people filled the futuristic Dulles terminal building. It was midmorning, and the pace of arrivals and departures had accelerated. There was the usual mélange of businessmen, politicians, vacationers, parents with children, servicemen, and others at the terminal. They hurried to and from planes and ticket counters, each concentrating on individual destinations, each more or less oblivious of the surrounding mass of humanity. For Joseph Banker, this fact played in very well with his plans. He tugged at the pilot's uniform he was wearing. It was a little tight under the arms, but all in all, he knew he cut a good figure and looked quite convincing. Carrying his flight bag, he headed toward the door that led to one of the flight-crew ready rooms. The guard at the door glanced at the blue pass pinned onto Banker's lapel, smiled, then let Banker through the door.

Banker relaxed somewhat. That was just about the last obstacle. He hurried down the corridor and into a flight-crew locker room. The room was empty. Banker wouldn't have cared if there were other pilots there, however. He was wearing the uniform of the world's largest airline. Even if he met a pilot of the same company, it wouldn't have seemed strange if the other pilot didn't know him. It was this kind of planning in depth that made Banker feel very, very secure about this whole operation.

Banker counted down the row of lockers, found locker 17A. He quickly unlocked it and took out a maintenance man's uniform that was hanging on a hook there. He hurried into the rest room that adjoined the locker area.

Inside the stall that was farthest from the door, Banker quickly changed from the pilot's uniform into the white coveralls of a maintenance man. He hurriedly stuffed the pilot's uniform into his flight bag. He heard the sound of someone enter the rest room. He waited patiently for the man to take care of his business and leave. Then Banker lifted the lid from the toilet tank in his stall. Inside, floating on the water in an airtight plastic bag was a .45-caliber automatic. He removed the gun, tucked it into his coverall pocket, and left the rest room.

Banker locked the flight bag that contained his pilot's uniform in the locker. He turned to the wall mirror and inspected his new appearance. To all intents and purposes he now was just another airport maintenance man. However, he quickly realized that something was missing. Banker reached into the coverall pocket and took out a plastic identification badge. He clipped it to the lapel of his coveralls. The badge read: STEVENS PROJECT—CLEARANCE TO HANGAR C. Banker checked his watch. Smiling, he headed out the door that led to the field. Things were going very well.

After the 747 was towed into the hangar, it was surrounded by swarms of workmen and maintenance crews. Now that the final air test of the plane had been made, the loading process could begin. A steady stream of trucks entered the hangar, discharged their contents, then left.

The plane was surrounded by service trucks. Parked among them were two armored cars that contained cases of paintings and sculptures. This was part of Philip Stevens' art collection. It would be loaded on the 747 and brought to Palm Beach tonight, for display in Stevens' museum.

Gallagher and Buchek watched as cases were opened and paintings were transferred to specially designed aluminum cargo containers. Padded slots in the containers held the paintings securely so they could make the flight without any possibility of damage. As a case was filled, it was placed on a hydraulic lift and raised to the plane's cargo doors for storage in the 747's huge cargo compartments.

As Gallagher looked on, Utrillos, Van Goghs, and several impressionist works were transferred carefully to a cargo container. He turned to Buchek and, smiling, asked, "Which is worth more, the cargo or the plane?"

"I don't know," Buchek replied. "At this point it's a toss-up." Laughing, the two men crossed to the next loading area, where catering trucks were already arriving. They transferred their goods to waiting hydraulic pallets. It wasn't the usual sort of airline fare. Iced cases of beluga caviar, large assortments of French cheeses, fine crystal, and china dinnerware all waited to be stowed in the 747's galley. A stack of open wine cases was moved onto a pallet to be loaded. Curious, Gallagher reached into one of the boxes and took out a wine bottle. He looked at the label with surprise, then turned to a wine steward who was nearby making an inventory of the boxes.

"Lafite-Rothschild, 1945. I didn't know there was any of this left."

The wine steward nodded. "That's what most people think—and after tonight, there won't be, Captain."

Gallagher carefully replaced the bottle in its case. The last time he had seen this vintage in a store, it was priced at $240 a bottle. Who but Philip Stevens could afford to offer it casually as one of the wines on a short air flight?

Gallagher noticed that Buchek was visibly beginning to relax. Although there was still much to be done, things seemed to be going along smoothly.

Buchek and Gallagher crossed the hangar floor to join a maintenance man who was checking the braking system on the 747's landing gear. As they did so, Gallagher looked across the hangar and spotted Eve Clayton, who was hard at work at a desk along the far wall of the hangar. Even at that distance, Gallagher thought, she was a damned attractive woman.

Eve was too busy, working at her desk, to notice that

Gallagher was observing her. She'd been delayed that morning and now had a lot of work to catch up on. Like Buchek, for her today was not an ordinary day. She had been on the project for more than a year, and today was both a culmination and something of an ordeal for her. She quickly went through the sheaf of waybills, guest lists, and notes of things to be done. The material was well organized in order of priority, and she was pleased. The papers had been arranged by her secretary, Julie Denton. Although the girl was new, she was very very good.

Organizing her thoughts, Eve went through the list of things to be done before the flight, her face a mask of total concentration. She was a woman of great beauty, with close-cropped auburn hair and a tall model quality that made men turn their heads when she passed. Yet, she was so self-possessed and confident that no one was greatly surprised upon learning for the first time, that Eve was a major executive with the Stevens Corporation. She was, as a matter of fact, Stevens' good right arm as well as his confidante. Their long association had justifiably made him reliant on her skills as a businesswoman and her discretion as a friend.

Dimly, Eve became aware of the phone bell as she concentrated on her work. She always found it annoying to abruptly refocus her energies and break her chain of concentration. However, after she picked up the phone and recognized the person on the other end of the line, a broad smile broke out on her face and warmth filled her voice. She was talking to Philip Stevens.

"Eve, how are you? Is everything going well?"

"Philip, it's good to hear from you. We're right on schedule. I'm watching them load the plane now. It's magnificent."

"And what about the guests?"

Eve laughed. "Who in their right mind would say no to a trip like this? Almost everyone's accepted."

There was a short silence on the other end of the phone. She knew that Philip Stevens, a man who never flinched from reality, was now trying to muster the courage to ask a single question.

"Eve, did you talk to Lisa?"

Instantly she decided that it was best to tell him the unvarnished truth. As painful as it was, she knew she owed him that.

"She's not coming, Philip. I'm sorry." She could almost feel the pain her words inflicted on him. She wished she could tell him differently, but Eve's long argument with Lisa that afternoon had yielded nothing new in the long-held breach between Philip Stevens and his daughter. If anything, it had reawakened Lisa's old anger at her father for his opposing her marriage, and, for what she called, not untruthfully, his trying to control her life. There was no way to convince her to join the group that was flying to Palm Beach that evening. Unfortunately, Eve thought, she had, at the end of the conversation, lost her temper. She liked Lisa, but sometimes Lisa acted more like a spoiled child than a young woman. Eve had pointedly told Lisa that even if she refused to see her father, Philip Stevens was at least entitled to see his grandson. It was a point that struck home, and Lisa quieted. But, unfortunately, she remained adamant about the flight. She wasn't going.

Philip Stevens listened to Eve. After she finished talking, there was a long pause. As if he were digesting her words, bitter as they were. Finally he spoke. There was pain and confusion in his voice. For the first time Eve could remember, he sounded like an old man.

"I hoped it would be different this time. I hoped the bitterness was over. . . ."

Eve tried to be encouraging. "She's still your daughter. I know that underneath all that anger, she loves you. There'll be other times."

"Let's not kid ourselves, Eve. There won't be other times," Philip Stevens said harshly. "I know how long I've got, and so do you."

Eve gripped the phone tightly and bit her lip. It was

25

almost a secret between them, but a secret she would have gladly forgotten, and each time she was reminded that Stevens had an inoperable cancer, she had to fight the wave of sadness that engulfed her.

"Philip, let me tell her. If she knew, perhaps—"

"The last thing I want is pity." Stevens' tone was decisive, and from long experience Eve knew she could not change his mind. "Look," he said, "I'll see you here tonight. And thanks—thanks for everything."

"All right, Philip. Good-bye."

There was a click on the other end of the line. Eve placed the phone back in its cradle. Before the call, she had felt full of energy; now she leaned with both elbows on the portable desk. She rubbed her hand across her eyes.

"Tired?"

Eve looked up. She smiled. Standing before her was Don Gallagher.

"You know it," Eve said.

Gallagher looked at her warmly.

"Let's go over to the office and have a cup of coffee," he said.

Eve raised an eyebrow and looked at him quizzically.

"You know there's no coffee in the office."

Gallagher smiled. "That's right, but let's go over there anyway."

Eve laughed out loud. He put his arm around her shoulders, and together they walked toward the project office, a temporary metal building that had been erected along the far wall of the hangar.

Banker walked toward the hangar with a relaxed and easy gait. The maintenance man's coveralls fit much better than the airline pilot's uniform had, he thought. Banker was the sort of person who concerned himself more with the details of an operation than with the larger aspects. He was always sure that if the details were handled properly, the overall plan would take care of itself.

Outside the hangar, Chambers, the copilot of the 747, was nervously waiting for him. Banker smiled. He considered himself a professional, and the closer they came to the job, the cooler he became. Chambers, on the other hand, was quite clearly terrified. They had been lucky, Banker thought, to have gotten hold of Chambers. Chambers had been flying the Los Angeles–Las Vegas run for one of the big commercial carriers. He had had plenty of time to accumulate a gambling debt that would have killed the average man. In fact, the people to whom he owed the debt would have killed Chambers. That was when Banker and his friends stepped in. They gladly paid the markers. They had a use for an airline copilot who would be completely in their power.

"Calm down," Banker said to the sweating Chambers. "Things are going to be very easy."

"I hope so," Chambers replied. "Wilson's already inside. He said to tell you that everything's going as planned."

Banker nodded. "What about the stuff?"

Frightened, Chambers looked around. The area was clear. He lowered his voice. "We got it in this morning."

Banker looked at his watch. "I better get moving."

He headed toward the doors to the hangar.

Chambers followed him nervously. "Watch yourself. Gallagher and Buchek are still in there."

Smiling, Banker tapped the yellow security badge that was pinned to his lapel.

"What are you worried about? I just work here. Remember?"

Banker turned and headed into the hangar, leaving the worried Chambers behind.

In fact, there wasn't any coffee in the project office. But Gallagher knew that Buchek had hidden a bottle of Scotch somewhere. After rummaging through the file cabinets, he finally found it. Now he and Eve sat, quietly sipping their drinks. The last few days had been too hectic for the two of them to see much of each other. Gallagher knew that Eve was happy to see him, yet something indefinable seemed to be bothering her. He sensed a certain sadness on her part that was quite unlike the Eve he had come to know. Finally he spoke, joking to try to break the ice.

"My problem is, I'm afraid of flying. What's yours?"

Eve smiled, but shook her head sadly and said nothing.

He tried again. "Eve, my darling, we've lived happily in sin longer than most people have been miserably married. When you have a problem, I know it."

Unhappily, Eve finished her drink and turned to him. "Don, Stevens wants me to take over the Geneva office."

Gallagher wasn't surprised. He knew that Eve was a brilliant executive and that she was destined to reach the heights in the Stevens Corporation.

"I'm a senior pilot," he said. "I'll just get a job flying the New York-to-Paris-to-Geneva route. That should be no problem."

Eve's spirits didn't brighten.

"Don, that means we'll see each other only one day, or, at the most, twice a week."

Gallagher thought for a moment.

"Do you know of a sounder basis for a happy marriage?"

Eve looked at him levelly. She knew that the fears she held in the deepest part of her heart would have to be made bare. She was afraid of losing this man, but there was a part of her that was afraid of keeping him, too.

"Don, I've already been through one divorce. I don't want the risk, or the responsibility, for another one, I guess. Can't we keep things as they are? For a while, anyway."

Gallagher finished his drink and shrugged. "No, because nothing stays the same. It's a rule of life. Things either change, or they die. But I think we better defer this conversation about our destinies for a little while. We've both got a lot of responsibilities today. We can talk about this in Palm Beach, after the flight. Okay?"

Eve nodded agreement, then crossed the room and kissed him lightly on the lips.

"Destiny later. But right now, why don't you buy me lunch?"

He took her in his arms. "Sold," he replied. "Let's collect Buchek and drive in to town."

4

Banker had no problem entering the hangar. Chambers had gotten him a security badge, and the guard on duty at the entrance had merely glanced at it and waved him through. Once inside, he quickly made his way to the 747, climbed the temporary boarding ramp, then entered the cargo compartment. From there it was a few steps into the kitchen area, where he knew Wilson would be waiting for him.

When Banker entered the kitchen, Wilson was stacking crystal glassware in a specially designed compartment. Wilson stowed the last of the glasses, then nodded to Banker and headed forward in the plane. Wilson was a heavier man, somewhat short, with closely cropped hair. Like Banker, he was dressed in maintenance-man's coveralls. Wilson reached into a service cupboard and took out a small toolbox. Then, followed by Banker, he headed up the stairs into the passenger level of the aircraft.

It was dark and quiet in the 747's passenger level. The cleaning crew wasn't due to inspect the passenger areas for several hours, so only the emergency lights were on in this area. Wilson headed toward a dark corridor at the back of the plane. Before he entered it, he reached into his toolbox, took out a flashlight, and snapped it on. Together Banker and Wilson made their way down the corridor to the very rear of the plane.

A small closet at the rear of the corridor contained a ladder. As Wilson held the light, Banker removed the ladder, then fixed its legs into receptacles that had been built into the corridor's side. Climbing up the ladder, Banker pushed away a movable ceiling panel, took the light that Wilson offered him, then climbed up through the panel, out of sight.

Banker had climbed into an area of the 747 called the plenum. It was a dark passage that ran the length of the plane, above the ceiling of the passenger areas. There, structural girders, air-conditioning equipment, and miles of wiring, vied for space.

A narrow catwalk ran the length of the plane in the plenum. Holding the light in front of him, Banker moved awkwardly down the catwalk, shining the beam of light from side to side, looking for the air-conditioning ducts. He grunted with satisfaction as the light found the metallic glint of the exposed ducts. He paused there, waited for Wilson to catch up with him. Then he traced the maze of ducts until he found one that obviously was the main air supply.

By this time, Wilson had opened the toolbox and taken out a small battery-operated drill. He began to drill a quarter-inch hole in the duct. As he finished, he hurriedly replaced the drill in the box, then carefully screwed a self-threading copper fitting into the duct.

Banker held the light patiently as Wilson did his work. Wilson was an expert at anything mechanical. He was a little too nervous, as far as Banker was concerned, but they had worked together before, and Banker had a reasonable amount of confidence in the man.

Wilson finished his work. A gleaming copper receptacle was now permanently attached to the plane's air-conditioning duct. Then he reached into the toolbox and took out a small green cylinder. Lettering on the side of the cylinder identified it as containing "CR-7 Gas" and warned that it was "For Military Use Only." Wilson attached the cylinder to the snap fitting on the duct. There was a small click, and it was in place, ready to pour its dangerous contents into the 747's air-conditioning system. He breathed a sigh of relief.

Banker turned to him. "Come on. Let's stow the guns downstairs in the galley."

Wilson nodded. "And after that?"

"After that, all we have to do is wait until flight time." Banker smiled. He had reason to feel confident. So far, the entire operation had been handled with ease and efficiency.

By seven that evening, somehow, all the preparations for the flight had been completed.

The sleek 747 gleamed under the bright lights that ringed Dulles airport, and a steady stream of guests had been arriving for the past hour to board the plane. Much to their delight, a red carpet had been stretched from the point where the shuttle cars arrived to the boarding ramp of the plane.

Don Gallagher had stood at the bottom of the ramp with Eve, welcoming the guests. But a half-hour prior to flight time he had to rejoin Chambers and Walker in the cockpit and begin the preflight preparations.

Settling into his seat, Gallagher switched on the radio.

"Flight service? This is Two Three Sierra. Any weather update since we filed?"

The radio squawked, then replied, "Center advises that heavy frontal activity off the Gulf Coast is continuing to build. You better keep a pretty tight schedule, Captain."

"Roger."

Gallagher clicked off the radio. They were in for a rainy arrival, there was no question of that. He listened to the cross-talk on the intercom and knew that the shuttle bus was approaching. These would be some of the last arrivals. He was sure they were, like the rest of the guests, filled with delight at the prospect of the trip ahead—as though they didn't have a care in the world. Ironically, it turned Gallagher's mind to the afternoon with Eve. Never had a relationship with a woman given him so much trouble. Or, for that matter, so much joy. But the time to think of that was later. Gallagher turned back to the flight console. He had an evening's work ahead of him. The decisions that had to be made between himself and Eve Clayton would be made in Palm Beach.

Inside the blue-and-white airport shuttle bus, Jane Stern tightly clutched the hand of her eight-year-old daughter, Bonnie. She watched as the airport sped by and they approached the 747.

"Is that it, Mommy? Is that the plane?" Bonnie asked excitedly.

Nervously Jane nodded that it was. All day, Bonnie had been pestering her with questions. Would they be leaving soon? Hadn't they better get going now, or they'd be late. That was at eight in the morning, when Jane and her husband, Tom, were barely awake. But, she supposed, she certainly couldn't blame Bonnie for being excited. The little girl had never been on an airplane before and was looking forward to the trip.

It had all started when Bonnie's third-grade class had read in the newspaper that Philip Stevens was turning his Florida estate into an art museum and donating it to the people of the United States. Together the class had written to Philip Stevens, telling him that they were going to draw a picture of their own and would send it to him for his museum. A month later, a letter arrived from Philip Stevens thanking them and asking if the class would like to elect someone to bring their picture to him—a lucky someone who would fly on the inaugural flight of the new Stevens 747 to Palm Beach for the opening of the museum.

Bonnie Stern was the lucky girl.

Bonnie's parents knew that there was no way they could deny the girl this special treat. But Tom Stern couldn't get away from work, and that left Jane to make the trip alone with Bonnie.

"Aren't you glad that we're going, Mommy?" Bonnie asked at least ten times a day in the week before the flight.

"Of course," Jane replied, but as the day approached, slowly but surely, she felt herself losing courage. The truth

34

of the matter was, Jane Stern had never flown in her life. In fact, the idea of flying was terrifying to her.

Now, as the shuttle bus stopped under the wing of the plane, Jane's heart nearly popped into her mouth. The thing was just so . . . well, so *huge!* Suddenly the fears that she had thought she was getting under control began reappearing. In fact, it frightened her just to be near the large plane.

"Mommy, come on, we're here!" Bonnie pulled at Jane's hand.

"Don't yell, dear," Jane said faintly.

As they got out of the shuttle bus, Jane Stern thought to herself that if it was so large, then it must be very sturdy.

"Yes, it must be solid as a rock," she kept telling herself over and over, until she remembered that rocks were also notable for a compliance with gravity and had a propensity, when in the air, to fall to the ground. She gritted her teeth as an attractive woman in a tan knit dress approached.

"Mrs. Stern? Bonnie? I'm Eve Clayton. Welcome aboard."

As they exchanged greetings, Eve looked over at Bonnie. The little girl was in white crinoline, and she clutched in her white-gloved hands the rolled-up painting the class had done. The effect was old-fashioned but charming.

"Hello, Bonnie," Eve said. "Mr. Stevens wanted me to give you both a very special welcome."

"We're really happy to be here," Jane said. She could see that a young man in a flight steward's uniform was waiting for them at the head of the boarding ramp. Jane Stern felt as if she were about to enter the dentist's office.

"It certainly is . . . impressive," Jane said.

Bonnie was tugging at her hand again.

Eve studied Jane for a second, then said, "It's your first time in the air, isn't it?"

Jane nodded.

As Eve led them to the boarding ramp, she whispered

to Mrs. Stern, "The first time I flew, I was just as nervous as you are. Don't worry, it's all right. You're going to have a terrific time."

It was exactly the right thing to say. There was an almost instant rapport between the sophisticated executive and the shy housewife from Towbridge, Maryland. Jane Stern smiled, and she and Bonnie headed up the boarding ramp. Somehow, things didn't seem as threatening to Jane as they had just a few minutes before.

At the foot of the boarding ramp a young woman wearing glasses hurried toward Eve Clayton. It was Julie Denton, Eve's secretary. She checked their names off the guest list as Eve approached. "Jane Stern and Bonnie. Right?"

Eve nodded. Julie positively beamed, Eve thought to herself. There was a youthful eagerness about Julie. It was an eagerness that so impressed Eve that she had taken the girl on as her secretary. That eagerness and a certain shy hesitancy about herself were both part of Julie's charm. She was the kind of girl whom everyone liked, but who always radiated pleasure and gratitude when she learned that someone liked her. She was attractive, with dark hazel eyes, a broad smile, and lanky good looks. But she was so unsure of herself that she consistently resisted Eve Clayton's efforts to get her to meet people. Even when Eve hinted that there would be some nice young men at the Palm Beach party, Julie had grown flustered. Eve had to smile to herself. She certainly had problems of her own, yet here she was playing big sister to Julie Denton. "Only thirty-five, and I'm already trying to play matchmaker." But then, maybe her efforts were having some effect. Eve had been so preoccupied with all the last-minute details of the flight that she hadn't noticed the striking red dress that Julie was wearing. She knew that Julie desperately needed all the praise and reassurance she could get.

"Is that new?"

Julie looked up from her clipboard.

"Yes." There was a pause. "Do you like it?"

Eve smiled. "You look terrific."

"Really?" Julie asked hesitantly.

Eve laughed. "*Yes*, really! Julie, you are impossible."

"I know I am," said Julie. The two women laughed, then quickly composed themselves. A chauffeured Rolls-Royce was approaching from across the field. As the long black car pulled to a stop at the red carpet, Julie checked her guest list.

"Emily Livingston, and that's about everybody."

Eve glanced at the list. All the names were now checked off, with the exception of Lisa, Mr. Stevens' daughter.

"Well, there's nothing more we can do about that," thought Eve as she moved across the red carpet toward the limousine.

Suddenly the rear door of the limousine popped open, almost hitting the chauffeur, who was approaching. Enegetically, Emily Livingston exited the car, with what seemed to be almost a leap. The chauffeur moved to help her, but she brushed him away, heading toward Eve at top speed.

Eve was happy to see the old lady again. Once more she looked at Emily and marveled. The woman never seemed to grow older. Short, plump, in her sixties—although no one had *ever* been sure just how old Emily actually was; yet, her face retained the qualities that had made her a classic beauty in her day. Now as an older woman, she had become one of the grande dames of New York society. Which meant that she had managed to outlive most of the people who, in the twenties and thirties, had linked her name in romantic scandals with, among others, Picasso and Hemingway. Emily felt that old age had slowed her down considerably. However, the truth was that she still maintained a pace that few younger people could keep up with. She was a veritable dynamo of energies and enthusiasms.

Emily hurried toward Eve, then gave her a delighted embrace.

"Eve, it's so good to see you. Philip was a darling to include me on this trip. I wouldn't have missed it for anything in the world."

37

"Mrs. Livingston, you look wonderful—I'm really glad you could be with us. Where's Dorothy?"

Suddenly a voice said, "Dorothy's right here, honey."

Eve turned and saw Dorothy approaching from the limousine. She was an attractive woman in her fifties and was carrying a heavy fur coat over her arm. Eve was happy to see her. Dorothy was a warm, intelligent person whose stories about the thirties and forties in New York always entertained everyone. She was a welcome addition to any gathering.

Eve couldn't remember a time when she had seen Emily without Dorothy. The two women were constant companions. She knew that, originally, Dorothy had started out as Emily's social secretary, years and years ago. But as time passed, she had become Emily's closest friend and confidante.

Concerned, Dorothy began wrapping the fur coat around Emily's shoulders.

"Now it starts," Eve thought. Amused, she awaited the explosion from Emily. The two women were famous for their arguments. It was well known that early in their relationship Dorothy had decided that Emily needed mothering.

"Dorothy, for heaven's sake. We're going to Palm Beach, not Siberia." Emily said.

"We're not there yet, and if you catch a cold, *I'm* the one who has to take care of you," Dorothy replied with mock annoyance.

Emily turned to Eve and said, in an amused stage whisper, "She's been mothering me for twenty years. I still don't know whether I love it or hate it."

"Wear the coat, Emily. Wear the coat," Dorothy said. She smiled at Eve, then gave her a hug. "Hello, Eve. It's good to see you again. Is this plane as fantastic as the newspapers say it is?"

"Let's go inside, and you can judge for yourself."

Dorothy looked to Emily and saw that she had taken off the fur coat and folded it over her arm. Giving Emily an unpleasant look, Dorothy headed into the interior of the plane.

Emily turned to Eve. "Now, if I get a cold, I'll never hear the end of it."

Smiling, Eve took Emily's arm and prepared to help her in the door. Emily found Eve's concern to be well-meant but basically unnecessary. Emily, as always, felt fit enough to climb a mountain.

"Now, Eve, I can always make it *to* parties on my own—it's afterward that I may need a little help."

Emily's outspokenness always amused Eve, and this time was no exception. She stifled a small giggle as she and Emily entered the plane.

Emily had been among the cream of wealth and society all her life. Luxury held no thrill for her. Eve wondered if the new 747 would impress her. But Eve didn't have long to wait. As Emily caught sight of the interior of the plane for the first time, her jaw seemed to literally drop. Amazed, she turned to Eve. "It's magnificent, breathtaking!"

Eve had to agree. "Breathtaking" was about the only word that described the 747.

Emily looked around. The center portion of the plane had been turned into one huge room. There was no conventional airline seating, and there were no overhead baggage racks. Instead, the walls went straight up to the ten-foot-high ceiling, providing a tall, spacious feeling inside the aircraft. Sofas and chairs were placed in pleasant conversational groupings, like the lounge in an elegant restaurant. Emily crossed to a couch and felt the soft glove leather. The dashing green stripe that split the center of the couch told her that it had been designed by Gucci, was made of the finest Italian leather, and probably cost a fortune. She noticed that the walls were finished in fine silk wallpaper trimmed with rosewood borders. One end of the room was dominated by a huge wall-size television set. At the other end of the lounge, a piano bar was set up. There, a pianist was playing light cocktail music, while the bartender served cocktails to the guests in Waterford crystal stemware. In all, Emily thought this main lounge was a room that would complement the most beautiful mansion.

Eve was delighted by Emily's reaction. She had gotten used to the look of the 747. She had been with the project from the day the first design was brought in. Then they had fought and argued as an overall-design concept for the jet emerged. From there, drawings became models, and the models resulted in the room in which they were now standing. Somehow, Emily's reaction made the work she had done all the more worthwhile.

"Would you like to see the rest of the plane?" Eve asked.

"There's more? It hardly seems possible."

"Oh, yes. The room we're in now is called the main lounge. Toward the tail of the plane there's a library, a communications room, a bedroom suite, a small dining room." Eve indicated a set of stairs in the forward part of the lounge.

"Those stairs lead to the pilot's cockpit. We've also built a small business office upstairs. Mr. Stevens and his executives will use that room to stay in touch with the corporation while they're in flight. It contains teletype, stock tickers, you name it. Directly below us are the baggage areas and the kitchen. We even have a five-hundred-bottle wine cellar so that our guests can have whatever vintage is their favorite. What do you think, Emily?"

Emily Livingston smiled, squeezed Eve's hand, and said, "I think I'm going to have one helluva time, Eve."

Emily looked across the room that was crowded with guests. She spotted three men seated at a green-baize-covered table. She turned to Eve. "I forgot my glasses. Is that Ralph Crawford over there?"

Eve looked and nodded that it was.

Breaking into smiles, Emily turned to Eve. "Something tells me that this is going to be profitable as well as fun, Eve." Giving Eve a wink, she made her way through the crowd of guests and approached the table. As she arrived,

40

Ralph Crawford, a distinguished middle-aged man, caught sight of her and smiled.

"I was hoping you'd be flying with us, Emily. Why don't you join us?"

Eagerly Emily sat down and was duly introduced to the others at the table. She sized them up as the introductions were made. Dr. Herb Williams, fiftyish, balding, overweight. Still, he had a twinkly smile and a confident manner. Emily thought she would probably like him. The other man at the table was a nervous, cadaverous little man. Emily disliked him on sight, and when she learned who he was, she liked him even less.

"Emily, this is Gerald Lucas, the noted art critic," Crawford said.

Emily gave Lucas an icy smile and extended her hand in a way that suggested Lucas' handshake was somehow unsanitary. Lucas chose to pretend that he didn't notice what was happening.

"I'm delighted to meet you," he said. "I admire your sponsorship of young artists."

"Unfortunately, I don't admire your attacks on them in your newspaper column."

Lucas froze. Haughtily he replied, "My reviews are never meant personally."

"Only a politician could have said that better," Emily replied. She was warming to the subject and was looking forward to a little verbal joust with Lucas, when she noticed the uneasy looks of the other two men at the table. Emily shrugged, saw a deck of cards on the table, and casually picked it up as she talked.

"Don't worry, gentlemen, I'll declare a truce with all art critics." She paused with the perfect timing of a natural-born comedian. "But only for the duration of the flight."

There was a moment of laughter; then Emily began to shuffle the deck of cards she was holding.

"Right now the name of the game is poker. Are any of you against playing a few friendly games?" The men seemed to have no objections.

"Fine. Five-card stud. Ten-dollar ante. No ceiling on raises, and nothing's wild. Las Vegas rules all the way." She paused and smiled sweetly. "Any objections boys?"

There were no objections, and Emily began to shuffle the deck in a lightning series of shuffles that would make any cardsharp green with envy. As Emily began to deal out the cards, she thought it might be fun to take that "damned art critic" to the cleaners.

5

Eve hung up the intercom phone. She had asked Gallagher if they could hold up the plane's departure for a little longer. But he had explained that it would be impossible. A bad-weather front was building down the Atlantic coast. They'd be fighting headwinds all the way. He didn't want to risk a late arrival. Eve understood his position. Yet, she wished they could just wait a little bit longer. Maybe Lisa had reconsidered and was simply late in arriving. It was a foolish hope, she knew, yet Lisa's presence would mean so much to Philip Stevens tonight. Eve was snapped out of this chain of thought by Julie, who, eyes flashing with excitement, came hurtling across the main lounge toward her. She leaned toward Eve and tried to whisper in her ear. But Julie's enthusiasm turned that attempted whisper into something that was quite a bit louder.

"They're here!"

"Who's here?" replied Eve, puzzled.

"Lisa, that's who. Lisa and Benjy."

Suddenly Eve's spirits soared. It seemed to be a miracle—but it was a miracle that Eve didn't intend to question.

Beaming, she hurried to the boarding door and arrived there just as Lisa stepped out of the airport shuttle car. With her was Benjy, her eight-year-old son. Excited, Eve hurried down the boarding ramp to greet them. Eve scooped up Benjy and gave him a kiss. He was taller and looked more like his grandfather than the last time she had seen him. The little boy squirmed with excitement.

"When's the plane leave, Miss Clayton?"

"We'll leave soon, don't worry, Benjy."

Benjy turned to his mother. "Can I go on board now? Please!"

Lisa brushed his hair back into place with her hand and nodded to him, smiling. With an exclamation of joy, Benjy hurried up the boarding ramp.

Eve turned to look at Lisa. She was a beautiful, leggy girl who looked younger than her twenty-six years. Her hair was the same auburn as her son's, and her bearing suggested an independence and strength of character. Eve noticed that Lisa was dressed a little too casually for this flight, perhaps deliberately so, if she knew Lisa. Impulsively, Eve gave Lisa a hug.

"Lisa, I'm glad you're here. I really didn't think you were coming."

"Neither did I," Lisa replied. The irony in her voice wasn't lost on Eve. She knew the old angers must still be burning within Lisa. They'd have to have a serious talk soon—preferably before the plane arrived in Palm Beach. Eve held Lisa at arm's length and looked at her.

"You look terrific."

She did look terrific, thought Eve. In fact, she looked wonderful. Eve thought back over all the years she had known Lisa. It gave her a peculiar feeling of nostalgia mixed with love. She had first known Lisa when Lisa wasn't more than a girl. Philip Stevens had done the best for her that he could do, but even with nursemaids and tutors, it was hard for a beautiful young girl to grow up without a mother. For the period of Lisa's adolescence, Eve had fulfilled the function of surrogate mother for her, and the bonds between them were strong and deep. Eve squeezed Lisa's hand.

"Your father will be very happy to see you."

Lisa's expression seemed to go from happiness to deep concern in an instant. It was as if seeing Eve had briefly made her forget a lot of bad feelings about her father—feelings that now were coming flooding back.

"He may be happy to see me, but I'm afraid it's not

mutual. I'm doing this for Benjy. He wanted to see his grandfather, so here we are."

Eve weighed this for a second. Then she shook her head, put her arm around Lisa's waist, and the two women went up the boarding ramp together.

"You know, I've just decided. You're really exactly like your father."

Puzzled, Lisa turned to her. "In what way?"

"Stubborn as hell—both of you!" Eve laughed as she escorted Lisa into the main lounge of the 747.

Lisa looked around the lavishly decorated area, then turned to Eve, somewhat astonished. "You can say a lot of things about my father, but when he does something, he always does it right."

Eve gave a smile of agreement, then led Lisa to a seat in the center of the lounge. The fasten-seat-belt signs were already blinking, and the passengers were readying themselves for the takeoff. Lisa called to Benjy, who was across the lounge examining the wall-size TV set. He happily ran to join his mother.

Elsewhere, the cabin stewards and the stewardesses moved through the plane, collecting glassware and helping people to find seats and strap themselves in.

Eve checked Lisa's and Benjy's seat belts. She looked around the main lounge and saw that the stewards were getting the last of the guests strapped in.

Belted into the chairs around the electronic Ping-Pong machine were Dorothy, Mrs. Stern, and Bonnie. Bonnie was peering out the window excitedly, and Mrs. Stern, though one could describe her as jubilant, seemed to be bearing up well at the prospect of her first takeoff. Eve was pleased to see Dorothy starting up a conversation with Mrs. Stern. That would be good. Dorothy could talk your leg off, but you'd be laughing all the way. Eve knew that that was just the sort of diversion that Mrs. Stern needed right now.

One of the stewards was helping Emily Livingston connect her seat belt, but the old lady insisted, of course, on doing it herself. Near her sat Crawford and Lucas.

Lucas looked as if he was happy the takeoff had interrupted the game. If Eve knew Emily, she was probably beating the man at every hand.

Over at the bar, she could see Eddie, the bartender, as he attached the last of the elastic restraints to the glasses in their racks. He gave her the high sign as he left the bar and headed toward the stairs that led to the lower deck and the crew seating area. Everything was okay. Two people were still at the bar. One, a slender woman in black with red hair, Karen Wallace. When Eve had greeted her earlier, she recognized that Karen had been drinking even before she got on the plane. Now, Karen's husband, Martin, a tall distinguished-looking man in his early fifties, gently took his wife's arm and guided her to a seat. Eve was glad of that. Something about Karen Wallace spelled trouble, and Eve was happy that, at least for the moment, she had stopped drinking. Sitting next to the Wallaces was Frank Powers. Eve knew only that Powers was Wallace's assistant. He was in his thirties, handsome, and very muscular. His build was the kind you associate with athletes, not scientists. Yet, she had heard that Powers was a respected scientist and virtually ran the day-to-day operations of Wallace's oceanographic institute.

Eve watched as a man in his seventies came out of the corridor that led to the back of the plane. He found a seat near the rear and strapped himself in. He carried a briefcase with him and was dressed in a beautifully tailored suit. Although his face was lined and creased with age, his blue eyes twinkled alertly, and Eve could see that the excitement of the takeoff was as invigorating to him as it would be to a younger person. He was an old friend of Philip Stevens'. His name was Nicholas St. Downs, III.

The twenty or thirty other passengers were in place and ready for takeoff. Eve wondered where Hank Buchek was. But as she was looking around, he suddenly appeared, coming into the main lounge from the hallway that led to the back of the plane.

Eve was amused. Buchek had spent the entire preflight period walking through the plane. He'd nod and say hello

46

to the guests, sometimes he'd even engage them in short conversations, but Eve knew that his real reason for strolling through the 747 was to look over his handiwork once again. Eve thought that he was just like a child who gets a Christmas present and then keeps getting up throughout the night to make sure it's still there.

Buchek waved to Eve. She motioned to him, and he came over to her. He looked immaculate in his new suit, and she knew that he had purchased it especially for this trip. He looked immaculate, but Eve noticed that his tie, in the interest of the occasion, was as tightly knotted as a tie could be, this side of a hangman's noose. Like many people who dress informally most of the time, his idea of formality, it seemed, was to be as uncomfortable as possible. As he sat down, Eve reached over and loosened his tie. Buchek breathed a sigh of relief. His expression said that it hadn't occurred to him that a tie could ever be loosened.

The head stewardess announced on the P.A. that the plane would be taking off shortly. Meanwhile, Mr. Stevens had a personal message for them all. The guests watched as the stewardess carried a videotape cassette to the wall-size television screen, then popped the cassette into its side. Instantly the screen lit up, and the face of Philip Stevens appeared.

"Good evening. I'm glad you could join us on this inaugural flight. I wish I could be with you now, but as you know, I'm in Palm Beach helping with the final preparations for the museum opening." Stevens' voice continued, and via videotape he told them a little about the museum and about the party they would be attending later that night when they arrived at Palm Beach. Lisa's son, Benjy, looked with curiosity at the image on the large screen.

"Who's that, Mommy?"

Lisa leaned toward him and tightened his seat belt. "That's your grandpa."

"Have I ever seen him before?"

"Once, when you were a little boy."

"How little?"

Amused, Lisa smiled. Benjy was at the age when his conversation consisted mainly of endless questions, and today Lisa simply didn't have the energy to supply him with endless answers.

"When we get to Palm Beach, you can ask Grandpa all those questions."

Benjy seemed satisfied with the answer. Lisa leaned back in her seat, her mind swirling with memories, all brought back by that familiar image on the screen. Behind her, she heard Emily Livingston say, "Look at him. He's just as handsome as ever."

It was true, Lisa thought to herself. His hair was gray now, his figure a little stooped, but somehow there was something rock-solid and unchanging about him. She realized that whatever that something was, it was beginning to make her uncomfortable. As Stevens finished his greeting, his image faded from the screen. The stewardess crossed to the wall-size TV and removed the videotape cartridge.

Lisa thought about her coming meeting with her father. Just seeing him on that screen somehow suggested to Lisa that she was still a little girl, and that made her angry. "Well," she thought, "I'm not a little girl, and I've proved that to him and to everyone else."

"Mom?"

"What, Benjy?"

"Grandpa sure has a neat plane, doesn't he?"

Lisa steeled herself against the warm feelings for her father that were, inexplicably, welling up in her.

"Your grandfather has a lot of expensive toys, Benjy."

The irony was, of course, lost on the little boy. But, strangely, Lisa almost felt guilty at what she had said.

"Maybe Eve Clayton is right. Maybe I'm just being stubborn," she thought. But those thoughts were broken by the sudden lurching movement of the plane as it began to taxi down the runway.

As the plane taxied into takeoff position, Captain Gallagher's voice came over the intercom.

"Good evening, ladies and gentlemen. I'm Captain Gallagher, your pilot. Mr. Stevens thought you might like a plane's-eye view of the takeoff. So keep your eyes on the television screen, and you'll see quite a sight. We've just received take-off clearance, so settle back and enjoy yourselves."

The wall-size television screen flickered into life again, and, to their delight, the guests could see the long stretch of Dulles runway that was ahead of them, brightly lit and gleaming under the dark Washington sky.

The guests watched as the lights of the runway flicked toward them with greater and greater speed. Suddenly the lights began to fall away and become miniature in their appearance. Now the screen was filled with the jewellike pinpoints of light that emanated from the city of Washington, D. C. There was a slight jar as the landing gear found its way into the fuselage of the plane. They were on their way.

The television view of the takeoff pleased Emily Livingston. She turned, in enthusiasm, to Crawford and Lucas, who were beside her, but she saw that Lucas' normally sour expression seemed even sourer. There could be only one reason, and for a moment Emily felt some regret. But, as she had seen, he was really as bad a cardplayer as he was an art critic.

Almost gently she said, "You shouldn't have stayed with that hand, Mr. Lucas. You see, I don't bluff that easily."

A raised eyebrow was Lucas' only reaction.

Crawford chuckled. That was just like Emily, a tigress one moment, then tending to the wounds she'd inflicted the next.

"He'll know next time. Won't you, Jerry?"

Lucas favored Crawford with a tight smile, then nodded. As a cardplayer, he knew he was overmatched.

Crawford shook his head, remembering the game and how it had been played.

"That was quite a hand, Emily. By God, isn't there anything you do badly?"

Emily thought for a second, then turned to Crawford.

"I've never been lucky in love. I notice you've discreetly forgotten about my three ex-husbands, Ralph."

"That's true," Crawford said, "but better to have loved and lost . . ."

"Yes"—Emily sighed—"repeatedly!"

Even Lucas laughed at that one. Then he, Ralph Crawford, and Emily Livingston settled back in their seats, ready to enjoy the pleasant evening ahead.

The 747's kitchen, cargo areas, and crew seating area were located below the level of the main lounge. Down there, the modern lines of stainless steel contrasted with the unlimited opulence that existed upstairs. Yet, there was still considerable luxury. The crew seating area, for example, consisted of airline-type seating that corresponded roughly to what would be first class in a conventional airliner. Now members of the crew waited there impatiently for the red fasten-seat-belt sign to blink off. There was much to do, and the service personnel were thinking about the jobs that lay ahead on this flight. Stewards and stewardesses chatted about mutual friends and other companies they'd worked for. Eddie, the bartender, was talking amiably with the chef, who tantalized him with tales of the exotic foods that would be served later on the flight. There was also an older man, dressed in a security guard's uniform. He was there as a formality, really. With so many valuable art pieces stowed in the 747's three cargo compartments, it was felt that some in-flight security precautions should be taken. He occupied himself by reading the daily racing form. He was totally unaware of the fact that two men, dressed as stewards, were watching him carefully, as if they were sizing him up—which indeed they were.

The two "stewards" were Banker and Wilson. Their minds were at ease. Putting the gas cylinder in place had been the last difficult part of the operation. The rest would go exactly according to plan—and the plan included a way of taking care of that security guard.

Banker and Wilson leaned comfortably back. This was going to be easy.

They had been in the air for more than half an hour. By that time, Steve Burroughs had been able to place most of the sounds and voices he heard.

He was seated at the small piano behind the bar, and, to the casual observer, the blind musician seemed to be totally concentrating on the endless variety of tunes that he deftly wove together, providing background music for the party.

In fact, while one part of his mind concentrated on the music, another part was taking in the sounds of the 747 and of the guests, as if he were orienting himself to a new world. That he could do this, and make music at the same time, might have surprised someone else, but to Steve it was an almost instinctual reaction. He had been blind from birth, and like most blind people, had developed an uncanny ability to remember people and places through a combination of sounds, tones of voice, and other characteristics he could hear. In fact, the totality of all the impressions he gathered could, for him, paint quite a vivid picture of the territory around him.

Through the myriad sounds of the party, he could hear a constant ponk-ponk-ponk. That, combined with the excited voices of children and an adult told him that Bonnie Stern and Benjy Stevens were playing the Ping-Pong machine. The adult's voice sounded like that of Dorothy, the woman who had come on the plane with Emily Livingston. In fact, near the bar, he heard the sound of cards being shuffled, as well as the sounds of laughter and of plastic poker chips being moved. That told him that Emily Livingston and the three men were still playing poker. In addition, he suspected that Emily was winning, since most of the laughter from that direction was hers. Beside him, at the bar, he had heard the impatient clink of ice cubes in a drink, then the voice that went with it. It was a woman's voice, low and

51

forceful, a woman who was used to getting her own way. Steve listened to the curt way that Eddie, the bartender, answered her when she spoke to him. Steve could tell that Eddie, who was normally very friendly, wanted nothing to do with that one.

Ahead of him, Steve could hear Eve Clayton in conversation with Mr. Buchek. He liked the sound of her voice, throaty and warm, with a directness that suggested honesty.

And, near the piano, Steve could smell *that* perfume again, and he knew that the girl had returned once again to listen to him play. He smiled, pleased that this was the third time in the still-young evening that she had returned. Steve found it interesting that each time she returned he found he would stop playing routine cocktail music begin playing songs that were meaningful to him, songs that he could put something of himself into.

He enjoyed an audience, but there was something about *this* audience that he especially liked. There was an intensity about the girl's presence that told him she was really listening. He played and smelled her perfume. He knew who was listening, and the fact that it was her made him feel very happy suddenly.

"You must really like music," he said.

Steve's voice startled Julie Denton. She had come over and sat down without saying a word. She had been listening to the music dreamily, and it had never occurred to her that the blind pianist could know she was there.

"Are you talking to me?" she said.

"I sure am." Steve shifted into a new key and segued into a bright up-tempo tune.

"I'm really kind of flattered. That's the third time you've come over to listen . . . Julie."

She was quite startled, and realized she almost felt as if she had been caught doing something wrong. Yet, she was intrigued.

"How did you know it was me?"

Steve laughed.

52

"Trade secret."

"Come on," Julie said. "Tell me, please."

There was a youthful innocence in the girl's voice. He recognized that, other than that, there was really nothing special about the voice at all. Yet, it made him feel very happy, as if it had some very special quality all its own. Steve recognized that it was ridiculous for him to feel this way. He had met Julie only twice before the flight. Once was when he had to go to Eve Clayton's office to sign his W-4 form. Eve had been late and while he waited, he had spent the time talking to Julie. They ended up going to lunch together and spent the entire time laughing and really having fun. The second time was just before the plane's takeoff. They'd exchanged no more than a few words amid the chaos of voices of arriving guests and last-minute instructions given to the stewards and flight attendants. Yet, the warmth of her greeting to him, and the way he felt, told him unmistakably that the potential chemistry existed for something to happen between them.

"All right, I confess," he said. "I remembered the way your perfume smelled, so I knew it must be you."

Julie laughed. "Steve, how could that be? I know I'm not the only person here who's wearing this kind."

"I know that," Steve said. "But you're the only one I'm interested in."

Which, he realized, was true. He hoped he hadn't said the wrong thing. He knew how shy she was. He could almost feel her blushing in the silence that followed his statement.

Finally she spoke. "I'm glad of that. I guess I feel the same way."

Her response took him so much by surprise that he almost stopped playing. But then he picked up the tempo, and no one except Julie could have possibly noticed that his playing had faltered. He could hear Julie breathing, and he knew she had moved closer to him. The breathing had a quality that was distinctly her own, and it felt very intimate to him. He realized that somewhere along the

53

way he had stopped playing cocktail music. He was playing his own music now, and he didn't know if it was for the party or for the young girl who was standing against the piano and so close to him.

6

Karen Wallace walked away from the bar, then sat down on a sofa—as far away from other people as she could get. She was bored.

The banter she had overheard between the pianist and Julie, Eve Clayton's young assistant, had ceased to amuse her. "My God," she thought, "was there ever a time in my life when I was as foolishly innocent as those two?" She supposed there must have been such a time for her, but if there had, she couldn't recall it. She had tried to make conversation with the bartender. He wasn't bad-looking. But after a while it became obvious that the bartender was simply not interested.

She reflected that it was a hell of a party when the only person she felt like talking to was the bartender. She looked around the lavish main lounge. Who were these people? She'd met most of them at parties at one time or another, she supposed. But who were they, really?

Karen finished the last of her drink, then signaled a passing steward for another. All the time, she was thinking only of her loneliness and of her boredom. Martin, her husband, was ignoring her on this trip. But how was that different from usual? "Important business," he would say. Bitterly she wondered if he didn't arrange to be so busy so that he could justify his inattention to her. "Research oceanographer," she thought. Just a title that impressed others, but meant he had a job that kept him away from home for months at a time. "What a life," she thought.

What did she want with him anyway? He was fiftyish, pompous, neglectful. Yet, there was some inexplicable thing that kept her from leaving him. Obviously, the same tie, or some similar one, kept him with her. Somehow, they had weathered all the fights and disappointments, and were still together. Why wasn't there some way she could communicate her boredom and unhappiness to him? Didn't he understand the pain and the loneliness that she felt?

But, no, Martin knew nothing of that. Nor would he ever understand.

Or maybe he just didn't care.

At that moment the steward returned. Taking the proffered drink from him, she began to move toward the corridor at the back of the main lounge. She felt her desperation and loneliness turning into a bitter anger. She hurried her pace as she passed the two children at the Ping-Pong machine. The high-pitched tone of their cries of excitement was, she noticed, terribly irritating.

Maybe Martin didn't care about her feelings. But if that were true, maybe she could do a thing or two that could make him react. As she entered the corridor that led to the rear of the plane, she thought that she'd at least let him know she was still alive.

Martin Wallace was thankful he had found this room. He was in the library of the 747. It was a large room at the back of the plane and contained a large desk and walls lined with bookcases filled with rare books. He would need all the time available before the flight ended, and even that much time wouldn't be enough. He leafed through the sheaf of papers on the desk before him. He was looking for the report on the undersea soil samples. Without even asking what he was looking for, Frank Powers picked the soil-sample survey out of the stack of papers and handed it to Wallace. Wallace smiled at Powers and took the report. This was so typical of their work together, Wallace thought. Powers was a gifted scientist, and, more important, always seemed to be totally in tune with him.

Wallace was confident that they would be ready for their presentation to Philip Stevens. Yet, this final review of their plan's details was a necessary preface to their meeting with him. If Stevens liked their project and agreed to fund it, Wallace's days of begging grants from penny-pinching research foundations would be over. But more important, if their plan went forward, it could result in amazing benefits to mankind in general. Perhaps they could even build some prototypes of the first seagoing food-processing plants. The possibilities exhilarated Martin Wallace.

But suddenly, a harsh voice interrupted Wallace's contemplation of all those pleasant prospects.

"You men are so lucky. I wish I had a hobby like yours."

Annoyed at the interruption, Wallace turned and saw that his wife had entered the room. She swayed slightly, spilling her drink on the carpet, and he knew that once again Karen was working herself up to an alcoholic scene.

"A plan that can harvest the seas for food, and save millions of people from starving, can hardly be called a hobby."

Karen bent low in a mock bow of apology. She mocked his tone and his English accent.

"I am so so sorry. I didn't mean to offend. I'm so bored, I had to find a little hobby of my own tonight."

Puzzled, Wallace turned to her.

"What hobby?"

Smiling, Karen opened her purse and began taking out a collection of miniature airline liquor bottles.

"See, Martin? Mini-margaritas, teeny martinis. Aren't they cute?"

Holding up a tiny gin bottle, she moved toward him. "Look at this one, Martin. It's about your size, isn't it? Maybe *that's* why I'm so bored."

An expression of distaste was frozen on Martin Wallace's face. Trying to control his anger, he quickly gathered up the papers he'd been studying.

"I'd better put these with the rest of the material. Excuse me."

Almost trembling with anger, Wallace left the room, closing the door behind him.

Karen crossed to Frank, ruffled his hair with her hand, then began to trace the outline of his well-developed arm muscles. He shook his head as he watched her play idly with his arm. Reaching for a cigarette, he moved subtly away from her.

With a smile, Karen raised her eyebrow. "Touché. I'm mean to him, you're mean to me. I forgot that you two are blood brothers."

"Why do you treat him that way?"

"What way?"

Anger was in Frank's voice now.

"Goddammit, you know how concerned he is about you."

Karen smiled, moved closer to Frank.

"I'm concerned about him. I'm more concerned about him than you are. You're the one who seduced his wife, you know."

Frank had been expecting this. It was the one thing she inevitably brought up to use against him. It was something he was ashamed of.

"I remember. I wish to God I didn't, Karen."

Karen took a slow drink, then looked at Frank with a measured glance.

"I'm lonely. I need somebody to be nice to me this week. Can you be nice to me this week?"

"What if I can't?"

Karen shrugged. "What do you think Martin would say if he knew about us? I really don't think he'd mind. Why don't I ask him?"

Frank almost laughed. She was more than just a calculating bitch, she was crazy. Perhaps, he feared, she was crazy enough to carry out that threat.

"So you're blackmailing me?"

Karen nodded in the affirmative, smiling sweetly for the first time. "Yes, I am. Who else have I got to blackmail? I don't get to fool around a lot."

She blew a mocking kiss at Frank. "I'll see you in Palm Beach."

She left the room, closing the door behind her. Angry, Frank sat down and stubbed out his cigarette in an ashtray. He really didn't know what he was going to do.

7

The door to the cockpit opened, and Eve Clayton came in, bearing a tray that contained three coffeecups.

"I thought you gentlemen might like some coffee."

Walker, the flight engineer, smiled, reached over, and took a cup.

"You read my mind."

Eve offered a cup to Chambers, the copilot, who took it noncommittally.

Gallagher had his headset on and was in communication with Palm Beach. As he talked, he turned and motioned Eve to come closer.

"Eve Clayton just came in. I think she has a message for you, Mr. Stevens."

Eve leaned down next to Gallagher, and he placed the headset over her ears. For a second she was conscious of the way his hands felt as they brushed by her hair, and the warmth was pleasing to her. Then the hands were gone, and she was talking to Philip Stevens. Excited, she told him the good news without even saying hello first.

"Philip, Lisa and Benjy are on the plane!"

All Eve could hear on the headphones was a brief sigh—whether of gratitude, relief, or joy, she could not tell.

Finally Stevens spoke, his voice filled with emotion. "That's wonderful, Eve! I don't know how you did it, but thank you!"

"But that's the best part, Philip. You don't have to thank me. She decided to come on her own."

"I'll be waiting for you at the airport."

"I'll see you there, Philip."

Eve took off the headset and gave it back to Gallagher. As he took it, he let his hand linger on hers. He smiled,

59

and as Eve returned the smile, she felt all the old warmth that she felt for Don come flooding back into her. Gallagher put the headset back on and turned to his work. Eve stayed there, letting her hand rest on his shoulder. She felt vulnerable with these feelings. She wished she could isolate them, file them away, deal with them in the strict and efficient manner with which she dealt with the myriad daily problems that confronted her as an executive of the Stevens Corporation. It would have been so easy then: she could make her decision and never see Don Gallagher again. It would then be as cut-and-dried as she had presented it to Gallagher that afternoon. But of course, it wasn't, and as usual, Gallagher had forced her into realizing that. She also realized that when she made her decision about their future, it would be a decision of flesh and blood. But that's the way it had been between them from the start, difficult and painful, but oh so very special.

Finally she spoke.

"I've been thinking about what you said before."

Gallagher looked up at her.

"So have I."

"I want to see you in Palm Beach," Eve said.

Gallagher reached up and put his hand over hers.

"I think that can be arranged," he said.

There was a warm lightheartedness to his tone, and Eve squeezed his hand. She stood there looking out the cockpit windows and into the night skies beyond. She could see the crystalline and cold pinpoints of light that were the stars. The 747 was far, far above the level of the clouds, in that atmosphere of serene calm that Gallagher had often told her about. Below them, she could see the silver rays of the moon as they spread over the carpet of cloud formations over which they flew.

Suddenly she understood why Gallagher had spoken with such emotion about night flying. There was a feeling about it that could be shared—but not explained. She smiled and squeezed his hand. She had better go back to the party.

They were due in Plam Beach in less than two hours. After that, Eve thought, they would have all the time together that they needed.

The red digital numbers flicked on, registered seven-forty-five, then flicked off again. Wilson noted the time, lit a cigarette, then took a quick drag. The wine steward had sent him down to the pantry to fetch more wine. He had decided to grab a few moments of relaxation. He puffed on the cigarette and noted how strangely calm he felt. Suddenly the sound of someone coming down the stairs from the main lounge brought Wilson to his feet.

It was Banker, who came in the door of the pantry. "Get a move on, the wine steward's wondering what happened to you."

"What difference does it make? It'll all be over in thirty minutes," Wilson said.

Exasperated, Banker shook his head. "This may be a charade, but it's a charade we'll play all the way. Now, get that wine upstairs.."

Wilson knew that Banker was right. He quickly moved to comply. There was too much at stake to take the slightest chance.

"I'm holding three queens, Mr. Lucas," Emily Livingston said. "Can you beat that?"

She spread her cards out on the green baize of the tabletop and looked Gerald Lucas straight in the eye. She had a strong suspicion that this pot was going to be hers. Lucas threw his cards on the table.

Two deuces do not beat three queens. Pleased, Emily Livingston raked in the pot. But as she did so, a uniformed steward carefully offered her a silver tray upon which was a single drink in a crystal tumbler.

"Champagne on the rocks, ma'am."

Emily hesitated for a moment, then took the proffered drink.

"Why, that used to be my favorite—but how could you have known?"

It was then that the steward handed her the elegantly engraved card.

"Nicholas St. Downs III," Emily read aloud.

She was thunderstruck, and her surprise must have shown, because Ralph Crawford stopped shuffling the deck of cards and looked at her, concerned.

"Is something the matter, Emily?" he asked.

But she didn't even hear him. Her only thought was of Nicholas St. Downs. Could it actually be him? She rose from her chair and looked around.

Seated at the back of the lounge was an older man. He was smiling. She recognized him immediately. Though much older, he was still the picture of sophistication and worldly charm.

"Nicky, it is you! I don't believe it!" Emily cried. Heads turned, and there were smiles as Emily raced toward Nicholas St. Downs. But she was totally oblivious of the responses of others. All that mattered was the tall man with wavy gray hair who rose to meet her, his arms outstretched and a vigorous smile on his face.

Nicholas put his arms around her, and they exchanged a warm hug. Still holding his hands, Emily drew back so that she could look at him again. He was just as she remembered him—the blue eyes, deep-set in the strong face that seemed to judge calmly; the lines around his mouth that formed deep marks when he smiled. And his voice, still that same magnificent voice, deep, mellow, and with the faint accent of his Southern upbringing.

She shook her head in wonderment.

"After all these years, you turn up here. Where have you been?"

Nicholas smiled. "London, mostly," he said. Then, his hand on her shoulder, he asked her to sit next to him on the sofa.

Once seated, Emily and Nicholas looked at each other for a long time before speaking. Emily felt her pulse quicken slightly. Such unabashed feelings made her slightly embarrassed in a way she hadn't felt in years. Nicholas was a face from the past. Yet, she remembered it all so clearly, it seemed to her that it could have all taken place yesterday. She had been just a naive young girl then, traveling the Continent. He couldn't have been that much older than she was, but to her he seemed to be the most sophisticated man she'd ever met. Together they had visited Scotland and the English lake country. It had been an idyllic time and touched a memory in her of the deep sensuality they had once shared. For a moment, she almost felt like a nervous schoolgirl, but then she recovered her composure, and their conversation took on the commonplace character of the reunion of two old friends. Still, it was hard to keep her thoughts from drifting back to that treasured time.

"You know Philip Stevens?" she asked him.

"It's difficult to work in the world of art, or the world of finance, and not know him," Nicholas said.

"And which world is yours?"

"Both," Nicholas said. "I arrange financing for a number of museums, and I have a nice art collection of my own." There was pride in his voice, but he stopped there. An unwillingness to speak openly of his own successes had, Emily thought, always been a deeply attractive characteristic of his. Emily reflected that there was a combination of strength and modesty in Nicholas St. Downs that she had never found in any other man.

Nicholas felt the warm feelings growing inside him. Now, almost to change the subject, he asked Emily if she'd like to see the gift he had brought for the museum opening. Emily nodded.

Nicholas reached down and brought his beautiful leather attaché case onto his lap. There was a smile on his face. It was a smile that he knew she would share, once he opened the case. He unsnapped it, then held it open for her view. Her reaction did not disappoint him. Against the black velvet of the case's interior rested two Russian icons. They were covered with amethysts, and the blue of the gems sent a shiver through her.

Nicholas could see her pleasure as she looked at the icons.

"Can you imagine," he said, "these two dazzlers mysteriously disappeared from Russia more than one hundred and fifty years ago. One was found recently in Japan, and the other in, of all places, Finland."

Emily lightly touched the two icons, then looked up into St. Downs's face.

"Together again, as they say in the movies."

"Together again," said Nicholas St. Downs, "is a happy phrase, Emily."

Impulsively, Emily took his hand. "Oh, Nicky! It *is* good to see you again."

A steward passed, and Nicholas deftly removed two glasses of champagne from his tray. He handed one to Emily.

"Then we shall drink to us," he said.

They silently drank the champagne. It tasted delicious, and when Emily brought her glass down, she could see that Nicholas was beaming.

"Do you remember that old castle in Scotland? I've never forgotten it."

Emily nodded. "We had so much together, didn't we? It was first love." She gave a gay laugh. "Thank God it happens only once. You have to be young and ready to take on the world to endure such despair—and such joy."

"That's true, Emily. That's very true." Nicholas took a sip of his champagne. "And now? Are you married, Emily?"

She shrugged. "At the moment, no. I've been through three husbands. They couldn't seem to keep up with me. And you?"

"My wife died three years ago," Nicholas said.

"I'm sorry."

Nicholas shook his head. "There's no need to be sorry. It was a long and very happy union. I have two fine sons and three grandsons, so far."

"How wonderful," Emily said.

She thought a moment. How strange it was. Not long ago, she and Nicholas had been little more than children themselves, with a seemingly endless number of years of life before them. And now, here they were, talking about Nicholas' own children. And, my God, Nicholas' *grand*-children.

"I wish I could meet them sometime," she said.

"Why not? Come back to London, and I'll arrange it."

He put his hand over hers. "You know, that castle is still in Scotland. And the countryside is as beautiful as ever."

Emily Livingston smiled. After all these years, Nicholas St. Downs was still a very powerful charmer.

"You know," she said, "I just might do that."

Outside the 747, the sky was like a peaceful sea of great tranquillity. It was true that, far below the plane, high winds and heavy rains were building to a storm of some magnitude. But, up here at 40,000 feet, the 747 was able to plow serenely on.

In the cockpit, the flight crew worked with quiet efficiency. The flight engineer, Walker, sipped coffee and chatted with Gallagher about the intricacies of fly-fishing. Suddenly Walker became conscious of a gauge on his instrument panel that was holding at a low reading. Walker flicked a switch, changing calibrations on the gauge, but the low reading remained. Concerned, he called to Gallagher.

"Captain, take a look at this."

Gallagher swung around in his seat, and his eyes scanned the flight engineer's panel.

"That's a bad reading for the middle hold. How's the pressure?"

Walker checked the pressure and air-supply gauges. Pressure to all the cargo holds was constant. He reported this to Gallagher. Gallagher nodded.

"Gauge calibration check out?"

"Yes, Captain."

"If the pressure's constant and the gauge calibration checks out, then the problem's got to be with the sensor.

Still, you can't be too careful. I'll ask Buchek to take a look." Gallagher reached for the intercom.

Buchek had joined Eve at the bar. He was nursing a glass of ginger ale and enjoying a pleasant conversation with Eve and Eddie, the bartender. The intercom phone behind Eddie rang, and he picked it up.

"It's the captain. For you, Mr. Buchek."

Buchek took the telephone, retreated to the end of the bar, and began speaking to the captain. Eve listened in on their conversation until it became so technical that she was lost. Once again she turned her attention to Eddie. Eve knew he was ordinarily a happy person, but today he had reason to be even happier.

"I hear this may be a special day for you, Eddie."

Eddie's reply was filled with excitement and happy anticipation. "Yeah. You know what the doctor said? It's going to be twins."

"Nervous?" she asked.

Eddie nodded. "I'm terrified—it's the first time."

Buchek hung up the phone. Eve looked at him questioningly, as if to say: "Is something wrong?" He waved away her fears. Actually, the replacement of what was certainly a defective sensor unit was of small concern. He had been enjoying his conversation and would have liked to remain. But Buchek was nothing if not conscientious. He downed the last of his ginger ale, then headed for the stairs that led to the power deck.

Watching Buchek go, Eve thought that she too had unfinished business. She turned to Eddie. "Have you seen Mr. Stevens' daughter?"

Eddie nodded. "She was in the office upstairs. I sent a drink to her a while ago."

Eve turned to go, then, almost as an afterthought said, "Eddie, why don't you go to the communications room and call your wife? I'm sure you're anxious to talk to her." She signaled to a passing steward. "Larry. Take over the bar for a few minutes."

The steward nodded and took Eddie's place. Eddie quickly hurried toward the communications room, thanking Eve profusely as he went.

Eve, a serious look on her face, headed for the stairs that led to the upper deck and the confrontation with Lisa that she knew was inevitable.

8

The upstairs office was on the flight-deck level of the 747 and was just opposite the cockpit. The office had been furnished with a deep multicolored wool rug and a large mahogany desk. The walls were paneled in burnished rosewood. Built into one wall were teletypes and stock tickers.

Lisa sat on a large leather couch and sipped a martini slowly. Her feet were drawn up underneath her, and she had kicked her shoes off. She eyed the teletype and the stock ticker wearily. They were silent now, but once the Stevens 747 completed its inaugural flight this evening, the plane would be turned over to the corporation for company use. Then the machines would operate constantly, noisily chattering away the heartbeat of the Stevens Corporation's global holdings.

It was a sound that Lisa had grown up with and had grown to hate. It seemed to symbolize the unceasing and frantic activity that had constantly kept her father from her when she was growing up.

She heard the door to the office open, and turned her head. Eve Clayton entered, with a smile on her face. Lisa was glad Eve had come upstairs to join her. She liked the older woman. Ever since Lisa had lost her mother when she was fourteen, Eve had taken on the role of big sister and had tried to guide her through the agonizing period of adolescence. But there was more to her attachment to Eve than that. The fact was that Lisa respected Eve's judgment, and saw an objectivity and fairness in Eve that she had found in very few other people. It was this respect that made it all the more difficult for Lisa to oppose Eve in her efforts to reunite her with her father.

Eve sat next to Lisa. She put a gentle hand on Lisa's shoulder. "You look terribly depressed. What is it, Lisa?"

Lisa sipped her drink and tried to collect her thoughts. She was experiencing so many conflicting feelings, it was hard to summarize what she felt. Finally she spoke. "I think I'm little upset with myself. Daddy calls, and little Lisa comes running. It's the same old story, isn't it?"

"Don't look at it that way. He's missed you so much. Two years is a long time, isn't it?"

Lisa sighed. "It is." She looked levelly at Eve. Now seemed the time for her to say it. "Eve, in those two years, I've tried to make a life for myself and Benjy. I've tried to become someone on my own, not just 'Philip Stevens' daughter.'"

"Lisa, you've done very well on your own. Everyone knows that. But don't you see, you've *always* been more than just Philip Stevens' daughter."

"Sometimes I think my father forgets that."

Eve had to admit that Lisa had a point. In the past, Philip Stevens had been highly possessive of his daughter. She could understand why. Lisa was Philip Stevens' only child. After the death of her mother, the teenage girl became Philip Stevens' only true link to real feelings. She was the thing he cared most about in life. And Eve could also see how the young girl had felt herself to be a prisoner of such love.

Stevens felt he knew what was best for the girl. Often he was right. But, justifiably, Lisa grew impatient with a father who obviously loved her but who was so consumed with the demands of his business that he rarely saw her. Rightly or wrongly, her impatience took the form of a stubborn denial of her father's wishes. An attitude that had led to the current long-standing breach between them. But, Eve thought, Philip Stevens had put his antagonism aside, and was reaching out for his daughter. Now it was time for Lisa to also call a truce. As Eve told this to Lisa, the girl just shook her head sadly.

"Eve, I know that all he ever wanted to do was help. I know that he's acted out of love. But he's a powerful man. He doesn't mean to, but he dominates everyone around him." Lisa sighed. "Especially me." She looked at Eve sadly. "I left home, intending to find a career and make a life for myself and Benjy. Well, I've done that. But my father hasn't respected my desire to be independent. His offers of money, the employees he sends around to see how I'm doing—it's all insulting. It's all his way of showing me I'm still a child." She looked defiantly at Eve and said bitterly, "But not this time. I'm going to make him understand that I must be allowed to live my own life."

"So you're going to Palm Beach just to have a final confrontation with your father?"

Lisa nodded.

The force with which Lisa had expressed herself made Eve apprehensive. She knew that there would be serious trouble after Lisa's arrival in Palm Beach. She had to divert this anger of Lisa's before the girl saw her father and said foolish things to him that she would later regret. Eve took Lisa by the arm and leaned close to her. She spoke gravely.

"This is an important time for your father, Lisa. Trust me. *Please* don't upset him now." Eve's tone was one of pleading, and it communicated the deep concern she felt at the possible consequences of this course that Lisa was planning.

Fiercely, Lisa reacted with all the years of pent-up anger and frustration that she felt.

"I'm going to tell him exactly how I feel, whether it upsets him or not. That's final."

Eve could see that there would be no stopping Lisa. The girl had worked herself into an emotional state that had to have a release. Yet, she knew what Lisa's words would do to Philip Stevens, and what the consequences of these words would be to Lisa as well.

Steadily, Eve told her the truth. In a sense, it was a relief to do so. Eve had been containing her own emotions about this matter and had had no possible way of relieving the strain that it had caused.

"Lisa, there's something you must know. As justified as your anger at your father may be, this is the wrong time to bring it into the open."

Lisa readied an angry reply, but something about the seriousness of Eve's tone frightened her and made her hold her tongue until she'd heard the rest of Eve's words.

"Your father's very ill. He needs your love and support *now*."

Lisa gasped a sharp intake of air as she heard this unexpected news. Then understanding began to dawn.

"Eve, the museum, the new charitable foundations, he's"—her voice wavered—"he's getting things in order, isn't he?" Eve nodded slowly and sadly.

"How long," Lisa asked.

"He has a few months, maybe a little more. We don't really know."

Lisa had always prided herself on being unflinching. But suddenly she felt dizzy, almost as though she were going to faint. Unsteadily she grasped Eve's arm.

"It's impossible," she managed to say. Her voice was almost a whisper. Then, breathing in deeply, she looked at Eve and said, almost defiantly, as though that would make Eve's words disappear, "It's impossible!"

Eve touched Lisa's hand gently. "I'm sorry, but it's true." She saw that the girl's eyes were like those of a hurt animal, uncomprehending, yet articulate with the pain she was feeling.

"Do you understand now, Lisa?" Eve asked. "He needs you—more than he ever has before."

Lisa tried to reply, but before she could form the words, large tears began rolling down her cheeks. Instead of speaking, she threw herself into Eve's arms. Gently, Eve folded her arms around Lisa and held her, rocking Lisa back and forth as though she were a small child. At that moment, the long-suppressed feelings about her father broke loose, and Lisa began to cry, with deep racking sobs.

Eve held the girl closer. "I know. I cried, too."

The two women held each other and cried together, both moved by their grief for a man they loved, whose impending death was certain.

Buchek stood inside the middle cargo hold of the plane. He had called Hunter, the security guard, to join him, and together they had moved several packing crates away from the bulkhead in order to expose the wall-mounted pressure sensor. As Hunter watched, Buchek took a tiny screwdriver that was clipped inside his jacket pocket and began to unscrew the gray faceplate that covered and protected the sensor.

Hunter had joined Buchek as much from boredom as from the regulation that stated that he had to be present whenever anyone entered a cargo hold. Hunter's job was easy for a man near retirement age. It seemed unlikely to him that they would experience any trouble wh the plane was aloft. And he knew that there would be other guards waiting at the Palm Beach airport when they arrived, so he didn't expect any trouble on that end, either. What that left for Hunter was a long dull trip during which he was stuck in the lower level of the plane. Thus, to Hunter, even the adjustment of a stuck sensor became an interesting way to pass the time.

Before becoming a security guard, Hunter had been a policeman. So it was no surprise that he was able to sense the presence of someone behind him even before that person said anything. Hunter turned and saw that Lisa's son, Benjy, was standing behind him, half in and half out of the bulkhead door. Hunter moved toward the boy in order to shoo him back out into the corridor.

"You shouldn't be down here, son," he said.

Buchek turned. He smiled when he saw the little boy. "That's okay, Hunter. Hiya, Benjy, come on in."

The little boy came closer and looked around. The cargo hold was strange new territory to him. Unlike the luxury upstairs, the cargo hold was strictly utilitarian. Benjy could see the packing crates and air-cargo

73

containers that were all carefully held in place by straps of elastic material. Here there were no rosewood panels to cover the walls. Instead, aluminum girders, interlaced with wiring and conduit, stretched from one end of the cargo hold to the other. It was just the kind of place that a little boy would find interesting.

Smiling, Buchek picked Benjy up and seated him on a packing crate. Buchek turned to Hunter. "I think the gauge is okay now. Close the door, and we'll check it."

Hunter nodded and moved to the heavy bulkhead door. He swung it shut and tightened the center wheel that dogged the door into place. There was a whoosh of air pressure as the door locked.

Surprised, Benjy turned to Buchek. "What was that? I felt my ears pop."

Buchek nodded. "That's air pressure. Each of these cargo holds is airtight when it's sealed."

Benjy seemed puzzled. "How come?" he asked.

Buchek tried to explain in a way that a small boy could understand. Still, it was hard to avoid becoming technical. The design of the 747's cargo holds was very advanced. Each was built so that its pressure and humidity could be regulated and be separate from that of the rest of the plane. In that way, art goods could be transported without the slightest risk of the conditions on the aircraft causing their deterioration. It was well known, for instance, that an Egyptian mummy couldn't be transported under the same conditions as, say, a Rembrandt. The Stevens 747 had been designed to solve that problem. Still, how do you explain that to a small boy? Buchek wondered. But Benjy was a very bright little boy, and Buchek was better at explaining things than he thought he was, because it wasn't long before the concept had gotten perfectly across to Benjy.

Buchek turned and picked up the intercom phone. He pressed the button that buzzed the cockpit and waited for Gallagher to come on the line.

"You were right, Captain," he said. "The sensor *was* stuck. How's the reading now?" Buchek was pleased when

74

Gallagher told him that the instruments now read perfectly normal. Satisfied, he hung up the intercom and began to replace the faceplate on the wall panel.

Benjy watched Buchek work for a while, then turned to the security guard. "Are you a real policeman, Mr. Hunter?"

"Sort of," Hunter replied, smiling.

"Have you caught a lot of crooks?"

"A few, but not lately," Hunter replied somewhat ironically.

"If I come back later, will you tell me about them?"

Hunter tousled the little boy's hair. "Of course, Benjy. Anytime."

Hunter saw that Buchek had finished putting back the faceplate. He turned and undogged the bulkhead door. It opened with a whoosh of air pressure. As the three of them stepped into the corridor, Hunter thought that it would be fun to tell Benjy some of his stories about his days on the police force. The little boy reminded .m of his own grandson, and he hoped that Benjy would come back downstairs before the flight ended.

It was eight-forty-five.

Chambers, the copilot, looked up from his watch. Although he knew that the temperature in the cockpit was regulated within a quarter of a degree of temperature, his body felt icy cold. He told himself to relax, to think of the entire operation as though it were the mechanism of a clock that, once sprung into action, would carry itself forward of its own momentum. In any case, it was a mechanism that was to be initiated at this precise moment.

Chambers cleared his throat and loosened his tie. His heart was beating heavily now; yet he had to seem relaxed and casual.

"It's about time I stretched my legs, Captain."

"Sure," Gallagher said, taking over the controls.

Heart pounding, Chambers eased his way out of the cockpit, closing the door behind him.

Standing on the flight deck, Chambers stood still for a moment, collecting himself. He could hear the merry sounds of the party filtering up from the main lounge. Then he heard the sound of footsteps mounting the winding stairs that led up to the flight deck. Chambers froze, then relaxed slightly as he saw it was Banker who was coming up the stairs. Chambers wondered how the man could seem so cool.

Banker studied him for a moment, then spoke. "You better calm yourself down, or you're not going to make it. You don't look good."

Chambers nodded. He felt sick, and it didn't surprise him that he looked sick also.

Banker thought for a moment. "If anyone says anything, tell them you think you're coming down with something. Have you got the keys?"

"Yeah. Here they are," Chambers said, as he extracted a key ring from his pocket. The ring contained three keys—one for each of the cargo compartments. Banker pocketed the keys.

"Okay. You've got ten minutes. The important thing is to get Gallagher out of the cockpit. I'll take care of that. But after he's gone, you know what you have to do."

"I know," Chambers replied.

Banker poked a meaty finger into Chambers' chest. "Good. Just make sure you do it." His grim expression suggested to Chambers just how Banker would pay off failure.

Banker turned and headed down the stairs. Chambers watched him until he was completely out of sight, then turned and walked toward the door of the cockpit.

Whatever would happen, the mechanism was now working. Steeling himself, Chambers entered the cockpit, hesitant but resigned to carrying out his part of the operation.

The party was in full swing.

After Martin Wallace had left the plane's library, he decided to go to the main lounge. Although his work was pressing, he found that the unpleasant scene with Karen had left him unable to concentrate. The emotional chains that bound Karen and him together were sometimes suffocating, and he found that now he just wanted to be with other people.

Soon he found himself talking with Julie, Eve Clayton's young secretary. Sitting near her at the piano bar, he had caught snatches of her conversation with Steve, the pianist. He smiled to himself, because the feelings he saw passing between them reminded him of feelings he had once had himself. In fact, he thought, not only did I have those feelings, but they were for Karen. He wondered where the feelings had gone, but had no answer. After he had been at the piano bar for some time, Julie began drawing him into conversation with her. It was refreshing to talk with this girl. Her openness and her ebullient spirit soon made Martin feel light and buoyant himself. He found himself explaining his work to her. Her interest and the intelligence of her questions spurred him on, and he told her much about oceanography and his intense feelings for his profession. Eventually he began to tell her about one of his private joys—scuba diving. It was his hobby, and it was something necessary to his work, but he spoke of it as if it were something akin to a religious experience.

Julie smiled. "It's wonderful to meet someone who totally loves the work he's doing."

"Yes," Martin said. "I'm very lucky in that regard." He paused for a moment, thinking of the many hours he had spent beneath the surface of the ocean.

"Can you imagine what it's like," he said, "moving with the current, exploring a world that's been hidden from man since the beginning of time?"

Julie turned to him. "I'm afraid I've got to confess something. Water terrifies me. I don't even know how to swim."

Wallace smiled. "You shouldn't be frightened of the sea. It's the origin of all life. It's wonderful down there." His eyes looked wistful. Almost sadly he said, "In fact, sometimes I think the only time I feel free is when I'm down there."

Suddenly Martin heard a derisive laugh next to him. He turned. It was Karen, and from the expression on her face, Martin could tell that she was looking for trouble.

"I don't mean to intrude," she said pointedly. Then, with a vicious smile, she turned to Julie. "Please excuse me, but could you move your ass, dear?"

Julie was shocked by Karen Wallace's words and by the raw fury she saw in her eyes. Julie rose quickly but with dignity. "Excuse me, please," she said to Wallace. Her cheeks flushing with embarrassment, she left.

For a moment Martin sat silently. His jaw was clamped in anger. A vein on his temple throbbed as he struggled to keep control of himself. Playfully, Karen drew a finger across his cheek. He slapped her hand down, then grabbed her wrist. His voice was cold with rage. "You miserable bitch. How can anyone be so cruel?"

She freed her wrist from his grasp. "And if I weren't cruel, how ever would people know how kind you are?" Her voice rose. Other guests were beginning to stare. She moved closer to him. "If I weren't such a sinner, how could you look like such a saint, Martin? Isn't that why we're together? And if it isn't, tell me—so I can stop acting like such an idiot."

Karen's voice broke. Yet Martin Wallace did not feel pity for her. The time for pity was past.

"Why should I tell you, my dear?" he said coldly. "And, as for acting like an idiot—you've become so proficient at it."

He got up and left her alone at the bar.

Hunter, the security guard, was in the crew seating area, eating dinner from a tray that had been prepared in the 747's kitchen. A steak-and-potatoes man, he found the elaborate French dishes strange but delicious. In fact, he was thinking about getting up and asking the cook for a second helping when something struck him across the temple and the universe exploded. As all consciousness vanished, he slid off his seat, to lie unmoving on the floor.

Working quickly, Banker tucked the lead-filled cosh into his pocket. He picked up a roll of adhesive tape he had set aside and prepared to tear off a strip long enough to cover the security guard's mouth. As he did this, Wilson, who stood at the entrance of the crew seating area as a lookout, noticed the odd angle at which Hunter's head was resting. Concerned, Wilson knelt down and felt for Hunter's pulse. He looked at Banker.

"Forget the tape. You hit him too hard. He's dead."

This information sank into Banker without making any impression that was perceptible to Wilson. After a moment, Banker nodded.

"Come on. Let's get him out of sight."

The two men half-dragged and half-carried Hunter's body toward the forward cargo compartment. At that moment, they heard voices approaching. They quickly pulled the body behind a partition that screened off an area where coats and wraps were hung. Leaving Banker with the body, Wilson hurried to the door of the crew seating area, hoping to intercept whoever it was that was coming.

The two children, Benjy and Bonnie, were in the corridor outside the crew seating area. They had searched the rear part of the plane, looking for Mr. Hunter. They had even looked for him in the kitchen, and been yelled at by the cook for their efforts. Now, the only place left where Mr. Hunter might be was the crew seating area or the forward cargo area beyond. Mr. Hunter had been Benjy's discovery. Now that he'd lured Bonnie down here with promises of Mr. Hunter's cops-and-robbers stories, he'd better deliver him, or Bonnie would think he'd made the whole thing up. Hurrying into the crew seating area, Benjy ran right into Wilson.

"You kids aren't supposed to be down here."

"Where's Mr. Hunter?"

"I said, you kids better get out of here."

In many ways, Benjy was as stubborn as his mother and grandfather. Hunter must be up front somewhere. He ducked around Wilson's legs and ran down the rows of seats in the compartment, looking for Mr. Hunter.

Hidden in the area where the coats and wraps were hung, Banker listened to the approach of the little boy. He weighed the cosh in his hand. He wasn't going to allow his plan to be jeopardized by any inquisitive little boy. He poised to strike.

"Benjy, Bonnie, what are you two doing here?"

Banker heard the woman's voice and pressed himself back against the wall.

It was Mrs. Stern. She had been looking all over the plane for the children and had finally found them. She called the children to her. Mrs. Stern was so relieved at locating them, she didn't notice how white with anxiety Wilson's face was.

"I hope that they haven't been any trouble."

"No trouble at all, ma'am," Wilson said.

Mrs. Stern herded the children into the corridor, then up the stairs that led to the main lounge. After she had gone, Wilson breathed a sigh of relief, then together he and Banker carried Hunter's body forward to a door that was marked "No Entry. Wheel Well Access Only." Banker unlocked the door, and the two of them placed Hunter's body inside, where it was unlikely that anyone would discover it. Banker locked the door, then consulted his watch. The children had cost them precious time. They would have to hurry.

Mrs. Stern had accompanied Bonnie and Benjy up the stairs and into the main lounge. The two children protested loudly all the way. They had been looking forward to hearing Mr. Hunter's stories, and Benjy, for one, couldn't understand why the man wasn't downstairs. He brightened for a moment as he thought of a solution. He would ask Mr. Buchek where Mr. Hunter was. After all, Mr. Buchek was in charge of the plane. Benjy looked around, but didn't see Buchek anywhere.

At that moment, Dorothy approached them. She looked at the two children with mock alarm.

"Where have you two been, anyway?" she said. "I've been waiting for a match with the two Pong champions."

The children broke into giggles and raced away, eager to have a match with Dorothy. Dorothy winked at Mrs. Stern. The kids loved playing the machine and had spent the first hour of the flight pleasantly occupied. Perhaps if they got them playing it once more, it would keep them busy for the rest of the trip. Dorothy and Mrs. Stern sat down opposite the kids, and the electronic reverberation of game machine joined the ambience of the party once again, as did the delighted noise of the children.

As the children played the elctronic game, all thought of Mr. Hunter, or his whereabouts, slipped from their minds.

Banker and Wilson passed through the main lounge and headed down the corridor to the rear of the plane. They attracted no attention, since to the guests they appeared to be simply two stewards heading purposefully somewhere.

Banker approached the door to the bedroom suite and stood by it, keeping watch. But Wilson continued on to the very rear of the plane. He was concerned because the time schedule had been upset. He had very little time left to get the ladder out of the closet, mount it, and enter the plenum. There, the green cylinder of gas was waiting for him. He looked at his watch. He had just enough time to get into the plenum and position himself for his part of the job. Just enough time, not ten seconds more or ten seconds less.

At the door of the bedroom, Banker watched as Wilson disappeared at the end of the corridor. He noted the time, then entered the bedroom.

The bedroom was lavishly furnished. The walls were covered with dark paneling, and their shade was reflected in the spread that covered the king-size bed. At the other end of the room, drawers and closets were built into the wall, and beyond them a door was slightly ajar. Banker went to the door and looked in. The door led to a bathroom, which was equipped with a stall shower. The room was empty. Banker closed the door, moved to the bed, and picked up the intercom phone from a nightstand alongside. He pressed the button that rang the cockpit. Gallagher answered.

"Captain, this is the flight steward. I'm in the bedroom. You'd better come back here."

"What's the problem?"

"It's one of the passengers, sir. He seems very ill."

"I'll be right there," Gallagher said. Smiling, Banker hung up the phone, removed the cosh from his pocket, sat down on the bed, and waited. He felt strangely calm and ready.

In the cockpit, Gallagher quickly got up and asked the copilot to take over. Concerned, he hurried out, on his way to the bedroom.

Chambers continually checked his watch. Everything had been timed exactly, and even nervous as he was, he still knew exactly what to do and when to do it. When the proper amount of time had passed, he leaned forward and flicked the switches that would put the 747 onto autopilot. Unsnapping his seat belt, Chambers reached into his flight bag, which was alongside his seat. He extracted a heavy .45-caliber automatic that was resting in the bag, and concealing it as best he could, got up from his seat and quickly crossed to Walker, the flight engineer. Walker looked up as he approached. He was just in time to see the heavy .45 come crashing down toward his face.

The .45 hitting Walker made a sickening sound. Chambers felt ill as he watched Walker collapse over his control panel. Walker groaned and moved slightly, and Chambers knew he couldn't take the chance that Walker might wake up too soon. Gritting his teeth, Chambers hit him again. And this time, Walker stopped moving. Chambers checked his watch again. The time was getting tight. He moved his hand toward the switches that controlled the plane's radio-telephone system.

9

Eddie, the bartender, was in the communications room. He had been really worried about his wife, and was, consequently, delighted at Eve's offer to use the radio telephone to call home. But, so far, he hadn't been having very good luck. When he had called the house, no one answered. That could have meant one of two things. Either his wife had gone out, or she had been taken to the hospital to have her baby. Eddie then made call after call, trying to find some relative who would know what was going on. But, for some reason, no one seemed to be home at any number he called. Even his father's business phone didn't answer. Keeping his fingers crossed, Eddie called his father's home, and was greatly relieved when he heard the click that meant someone was picking up the phone.

"Hello?"

"Dad. This is Eddie. I've been trying to reach Margaret, but no one answers. What's going on?"

Eddie's father was relieved to hear his son's voice, but this relief didn't change the gravity of his tone. "Margaret's in the hospital, Eddie. She's in very serious condition. Are you here? Where are you calling from?"

"I'm on the plane, Dad. We'll be in in an hour. Dad, what did the doctor say? What are her chances?"

There was an abrupt silence as the phone went completely dead. In utter frustration, Eddie tried to reestablish the telephone connection. But for some reason that Eddie did not understand, the radio telephone was not working.

Inside the plenum, Wilson felt cramped for space. His legs hurt, and he couldn't find a comfortable position. But he wasn't thinking of that now. He kept his eyes on his watch and counted off the last remaining seconds. Suddenly it was time. He reached beside him and picked up a gas mask. Fitting it over his face, he checked to make sure it was firmly and correctly in place. Satisfied, he reached for the green gas cylinder and quickly turned it on. There was a hiss as the gas began to rush into the plane's air-conditioning system.

Banker stationed himself behind the door of the bedroom suite, waiting for Gallagher to arrive. He adjusted the straps on his gas mask, making sure it was secure enough against his face. He held the blackjack ready, loose and carefully balanced in his hand. When he heard footsteps approaching, his body tensed and his muscles contracted, ready to spring. The handle turned, and the door opened slowly. It was Gallagher, and as soon as he was fully in the room, Banker swung, striking him a glancing blow. As Gallagher fell to his knees, shaking his head, trying to clear it, Banker quickly closed the door and snapped the lock. He moved toward Gallagher quickly, raised the blackjack, and brought it down toward Gallagher's head again.

Gallagher groggily moved away from the blow, grabbing Banker's wrist at the same time. Banker winced at the pain. The man's grip was strong, almost strong enough to make him drop the blackjack. Quickly, Banker used his free arm to give Gallagher a karate chop to the neck. Gallagher slumped, unconscious, onto the floor.

Breathing hard, Banker backed away from Gallagher's prone form. He again checked his gas mask, then looked at his watch.

The next part of the plan had already begun.

The gas entered the main lounge through the air-conditioning vents. The slight hiss it made was well covered by the sounds of the party.

Nicholas St. Downs and Emily Livingston were deep in conversation. As they discussed interests, travel, friends, they discovered that they shared more than just a past. They even learned that, oddly enough, each had individually visited a small winery in the south of France off and on for the past five years, yet they never had had the good fortune to cross paths there. They had Philip Stevens to thank for finally bringing them together again.

Nicholas reached over to the small marble-topped table that was in front of them. He picked up the open champagne bottle and began to refill Emily's glass. The glass filled to overflowing and beyond, the champagne spilling onto the floor. Emily turned to Nicholas to see what was wrong, just as his head sagged and the bottle fell from his hands, to land clattering on the table, then roll off onto the floor.

"Nicholas, what is it?" Emily reached out to grab his shoulders. But Nicholas' body slumped forward against Emily, and then fell, unconscious, over the table.

Emily reached for Nicholas, intending to help him. She tried to rise, but as she did, she felt consumed by an ever-growing dizziness. She tried to scream for help, but could utter no sound. She staggered, as breathing itself began to require a strength that was beyond her capability. Then she collapsed into unconsciousness, falling to the floor.

Steve Burroughs was playing the piano when he became conscious of a commotion at the other end of the main lounge. He identified it as being the area where Emily Livingston and Nicholas St. Downs were seated. At the same time, he detected an odd odor in the air. Cutting through the smells of cigarettes, liquor, perfume, and food was an odor that was vaguely chemical. It was a smell that Steve could only decribe as "menacing." Then he became conscious of a strange giddy feeling. He was aware that he couldn't concentrate on his playing. He heard discordant notes coming from the piano, then was amazed when he realized it was he who was playing those tones.

The discordant notes were so pronounced that the guests who were near the piano bar turned around to see what was happening. At that moment, Steve fell across the piano. A woman screamed, and guests moved toward Steve to see what was wrong. It was at that moment that pandemonium broke out. The concentration of the gas had grown, until now it began to affect everyone at once. Screams and terrified shouts filled the air, and bodies crumpled to the floor as guests fought to breathe.

Buchek had heard the screams. He rushed into the main lounge from the forward part of the plane and was stunned by the sight that greeted him. People were sprawled on furniture and on the floors of the main lounge. Even as he watched, growing numbers of people collapsed and were silent. Buchek's mind raced as he tried to understand what was going on. He watched, helpless, as Jane Stern collapsed near him. He saw that the two children had passed out over the game machine, and as Dorothy ran to their aid, she collapsed also. Buchek hurried through the main lounge, trying to get some clue as to what was wrong. What the hell is happening? Buchek thought to himself. What the hell is happening?

He saw the card players—Lucas, Williams, and Crawford—collapsed over their table, the cards strewn all about them. They looked peaceful and asleep. It was eerie. Buchek shook his head violently, trying to clear away the fog he felt enveloping his mind. His throat burned, and he now could sense a chemical odor in the air. He became aware that he somehow had fallen to his knees. He put out a hand to steady himself. He heard a voice—"What's happening? Help me. Help me!"—and it echoed over and over in his mind.

Everything was happening in an instant, he knew, yet his mind seemed to have slowed down, and everything he saw was happening in slow motion: Julie Denton, in a bright red dress, running past him, trying to get to the piano bar, then falling for what seemed to be an eternity, her body hitting the floor of the plane with a thud.

Buchek reached for her, then felt a jar as a steward collapsed against him, a tray of hors d'oeuvres spilling everywhere. He fought for consciousness and knew it was a battle he was losing. Jesus, he thought. He had to stay awake. He had to get to the cockpit and find out what was happening. But even as he was telling himself this, he was falling facedown to the floor, and the last thing he saw as his head fell were the bodies strewn across the main lounge. Curiously, the only sound that lingered in his mind was the faint ponk-ponk-ponk sound from the Ping-Pong machine. But even that soon faded, and Buchek fell unconscious onto the floor.

Wilson's pocket flashlight made a pool of light inside the darkness of the plenum. He held the light on his wristwatch as he tensely ticked off the seconds. The sweep second hand of the watch reached the top of the dial, and Wilson knew that this part of the job was done. He reached for the valve on the green cylinder and shut off the flow of gas. The faint hiss that came from the cylinder died in a sputter. Then, carefully making sure his gas mask was securely on, Wilson slowly edged his way along the catwalk to the opening that led down into the corridor.

Grabbing an aluminum brace for support, Wilson easily swung down out of the plenum. His foot found the ladder treads, and he expectantly stepped down into the corridor.

After being in the darkened plenum for so long, the light hurt Wilson's eyes. But as he made his way through the corridor toward the main lounge, his eyes began to adjust to the brightness. Breathing easily through his gas mask, he glanced into the rooms that were along the corridor, checking for any guests who might have retained consciousness. But there were unmoving figures in each of the rooms. No one seemed to have escaped the effects of the gas.

Wilson entered the main lounge. Guests lay everywhere. It was deadly quiet except for the sounds of the Ping-Pong machine, which continued its ghostly match, even though no player remained conscious. The sound irritated Wilson, and he moved to the machine and flicked off its power. Looking around, Wilson felt pleased. It was obvious that the guests never knew what had hit them.

As Wilson crossed the room, something caught his eye. It was the flash of gems, a heavy diamond bracelet on the wrist of the unconscious Emily Livingston. Wilson bent down beside her and felt for the bracelet's clasp. Those diamonds must be worth a fortune.

Suddenly, Wilson heard Banker's harsh voice. "Forget that. You're job's down in the hold."

Wilson turned and stood up. He saw that Banker had just come up the stairs from the lower level of the aircraft. Wilson pointed at the bracelet. "It must be worth fifty thousand bucks."

Angrily, Banker walked over to Wilson. "That's chickenfeed. We do this according to the plan. Now, quit wasting time."

Wilson backed away and tried to be conciliatory. "Okay, Banker, anything you say." Then: "How is it down below?"

"Just the chef, and he's out like a light. Now, get down to the cargo hold and start opening those shipping containers."

What was the use of arguing? Wilson thought to himself. Soon he'd be rich, and he'd never have to see Banker again. He headed for the stairs that led down to the cargo hold.

After Wilson disappeared down the stairs, Banker walked across the main lounge. He carefully looked for any sign of consciousness on the part of the guests. But, he concluded, there was no need for that. The quantity of gas they had used was apparently sufficient to do the job. And, as for any early risers, Banker was fully prepared to use the pistol he had tucked into his belt.

Banker quickly made his way up the stairs toward the flight deck. It was time to coordinate the plan with Chambers.

Banker opened the door to the cockpit and entered. Chambers was at the controls, his gas mask on. The plane was still on autopilot, and an air-navigation map was spread out before Chambers on the console. He turned and saw Banker. Chambers' look expressed the anxiety he felt.

"Don't worry, it's going fine," Banker told him.

He noticed that Chambers' eyes kept straying to the floor, where the body of Walker, the flight engineer, was lying. Walker's head was a wet crimson. Banker looked back at Chambers. He could tell that Chambers didn't have the stomach for this sort of thing. Banker smiled. Other people's squeamishness always amused him.

"Get him out of here, will you?" Chambers said, his voice choking.

Without a word, Banker leaned down and grabbed Walker under the armpits. It was difficult pulling all that deadweight. He dragged the body out onto the flight deck. Opposite the cockpit was the upstairs office, and Banker figured that would be a good place to stow the body. He opened the door to the office and dragged the body inside, leaving a trail of blood on the carpet. Banker let the body fall to the floor and stood up. He hesitated a moment, recovering his breath from the exertion. He saw that Eve Clayton and a younger woman were unconscious and sprawled on the couch. Banker thought that the younger one wasn't bad-looking. Then he placed her. It was Stevens' daughter. Some spoiled little rich bitch. Well, he thought, both she and her old man were in for quite a surprise.

Banker left the office and reentered the cockpit. Chambers had removed his flight jacket, and Banker could see the rings of nervous sweat around the armpits of Chambers' shirt.

Chambers took a navigation ruler and marked new course lines on the map, lines that showed a route that would take them hundreds of miles out of their original flight path. Satisfied, he looked at his watch and turned to Banker. "All right," he said, "it's time for us to disappear." Chambers took the plane off of autopilot, eased back on the throttle, and put the plane into a steep bank.

In modern aviation, the job of an air controller is a

crucial one. His major responsibility is to keep track of air traffic between the major airports of the country. With air traffic growing heavier each year, the nation's skies have become nearly as crowded as its freeways. It is the air controller's job to route and, if need be, reroute this traffic so that there are no collisions. To do this, the air controller makes use of radar, intricate computer links, and constant communication with the big planes, keeping a watch on every scheduled plane that's in the sky.

The air controllers for the eastern seaboard are located in a complex of buildings in Jacksonville, Florida. Run by the Federal Aviation Authority, this control center boasts the most modern radio and radar links in existence.

Inside the FAA complex is a large room. The room is darkened. One wall contains a map of the flight zones for the Atlantic seaboard, extending all the way down below the tip of Florida. The map has various markers on it, including the boundaries of the Air Defense Interception Zone, and other radar boundaries. Flashing on the map are the positions of the various kinds of air traffic in the monitored area. The information that regulates the position of the markers on this big map comes from the air controllers themselves.

The air controllers are a dedicated band who sit in the darkened room for long hours, peering into their radarscopes, paying alert and constant attention to the computer readouts generated in the upper-right-hand corner of their screens. These readouts are computer-generated elements of latitude and longitude. These, together with the complicated patterns on the radar screens, provide the air controller with the information that is the basis of his trade.

When the blip that marked the position of the Stevens 747 dropped off the lead controller's radar screen, there was an instant reaction.

Fear, raw fear for what it might mean.

The controller flicked switches that increased the magnification of his scope. When nothing reappeared, he put the scope in test mode, hoping there was some malfunction of his instrument.

Nothing.

"Jesus Christ," the man said loudly. "It's just not there!" He quickly turned to the controller next to him. "Jerry, take a look at this. I just lost Two Three Sierra."

Jerry leaned over and flicked the magnification switches. But, again, there was nothing. "You been having any problems with that repeater?" he asked.

The controller shook his head. "Of course not."

Jerry called out to a third controller, "I want a reading on Two Three Sierra. Last-known position was latitude N1500.° and longitude W08075.°."

As the third controller hunched over his scope, Jerry threw the switch that turned on the blue light on the status board. This let the others know that there was a possible emergency situation and started the chain of orders that could result in a full-scale alert.

The third controller hunched over his scope. He shook his head. "It's not here, either. Isn't that the Stevens 747?"

Jerry said nothing. He picked up a headset and immediately punched up the 747's communication frequency on his control panel.

"Two Three Sierra. This is FAA Control, Jacksonville. Do you read?"

There was only the crackle of static.

"Two Three Sierra. We have lost radar contact. Please ident."

But again, there was no answer.

Jerry's face reflected his bafflement. "Two Three Sierra. We have lost radar contact. Please ident."

Jerry looked up at his fellow controllers. They too were transfixed by the radarscope.

The disappearance of the blip from the scope and the unanswered calls could mean only one thing.

"My God," Jerry said to them, "I think we've got a downed plane."

10

Dense black storm clouds were amassed to the east. The Stevens 747 was heading toward them. The plane flew only a few hundred feet above the ocean's surface. The force of the aircraft's jetstream caused the water to roll and boil beneath it.

Chambers had brought the 747 this low for a very simple reason. At this height, the plane was out of the radar range of the land-based FAA air controllers and of the U.S. government's coastal-defense radar. Chambers knew that at this altitude the plane was untrackable. It was an ingenious plan, and one that, so far, was succeeding.

Inside the cockpit, Banker listened to the repeated queries from the FAA controllers as they came over the radio. After five minutes, it had begun to sound like a stuck record.

"Two Three Sierra. We have lost radar contact. Please ident." Over and over and over again.

Chambers leaned back in his seat and stretched.

"We're home free. We ought to be near the island in about twenty minutes."

Banker smiled. "There'll be no problem at that end."

Chambers looked at Banker. Like him or not, you had to admire the man's cool. There was no getting around it—Banker was some customer.

"You've got it all planned out, haven't you?" Chambers said. "A deserted island. An airstrip that hasn't been used since World War II..."

"And a pilot cooperative enough to help us out,"

Banker finished, his voice contemptuous. "Right, Mr. Chambers?"

Chambers clamped his jaw shut. There was nothing he could say to Banker. The man had him. Stifling his anger, Chambers said, "You just better make that transfer quick, before any of those people wake up."

Banker laughed. "They'll be sitting in an empty 747 wondering what happened to them. And we'll be halfway to South America, with a fortune in art goods. Take my advice, Chambers. Relax. Don't worry about a thing."

There is a red telephone at the FAA Air Flight Control Center. By using this phone it is possible, at the touch of a button, to communicate directly with the U.S. Coast Guard, or the U.S. Navy. This telephone is not there because there is a large number of air accidents. Instead, it's there because the rescue authorities realize that even a few seconds can make the difference between a successful rescue attempt and a futile one. As soon as the Stevens 747 disappeared from the FAA radar screens, a well-practiced ritual took place. And after attempts to communicate with the aircraft failed, the red phone was immediately used.

The call went directly to the Seventh Coast Guard District, which was headquartered at Miami and was under the supervision of Commander George Webber.

The FAA call was quickly flashed through to the Air and Sea Rescue Unit. There, the duty chief and the FAA flight controller quickly discussed the known facts about the disappearance of the 747. The duty chief, as he had been taught, asked all the questions that were pertinent: Had the last communication with the 747 indicated any trouble? What were the longitudes and latitudes of the last several radar sightings of the 747 prior to its disappearance? Had there been any divergence from the plane's scheduled flight plan?

As the FAA liaison expertly and quickly answered the chief's questions, Commander Webber listened in over the phone and made careful notes. He moved to a chart table and located the last-known longitude and latitude of the aircraft. Long experienced in air-sea search and rescue, he was easily able to listen to the raw data as it came in, and, at the same time, make immediate calculations as to the best methods of search.

By the time the phone call had ended, Webber had put the well-practiced procedures of search and rescue into operation. He had ordered two Coast Guard ships into the area and had sent a number of search jets hustling to the location where the 747 had last been spotted on radar. The planes would be hindered by darkness, he knew, and even though they had an approximate longitude and latitude, that still left a hell of a lot of ocean in which the 747 could be.

At that moment, Webber made a critical but wise decision. He wouldn't wait for the search jets to report back. Instead, he would start a full-scale search effort at once. That meant that, in addition to the ships and planes he would commit to the search, he would also ask the United States Navy to involve themselves in the northern sector of the search. That decision made, he turned to a seaman and asked him to get him immediate contact with the Navy's tactical coordination center at Jacksonville.

Although it was still quite early in the evening, Admiral Herbert Corrigan had already settled into bed. Next to him, his wife read a magazine. He was trying to concentrate on a detective novel, but his mind was already on the fishing trip that he was to take the next morning. Fishing was something he loved, and he had been looking forward to this trip for the last month.

His wife answered the jangling bedside phone on the first ring. She told her husband it was for him, and Herb Corrigan knew that something big was up. He was famous for his lightning temper, and among his subordinates it was common knowledge that tonight he was not to be disturbed. The call had to be serious.

It was. He carefully listened to Commander Reed brief him on what had already transpired in the disappearance of the Stevens 747. Reed then went on to describe the orders he had given already. Corrigan listened, concurred with Reed's judgment, then told Reed he would immediately join him at the tactical center.

As Corrigan rose from bed and hurriedly put on his uniform, he told his wife what had happened. She immediately went to the bathroom and packed his shaving kit, as well as a small overnight case. Being a Navy wife means being partly married to the Navy, and she was familiar enough, through many past experiences, to know that this search could last through the night, and beyond.

When she returned to the bedroom, the admiral was lacing up his shoes. He seemed deeply worried, and she thought it was unlike him. Year after year, she'd watched him carry out his duties as commander of the Navy's Tactical Coordination Center in Jacksonville. Every day, people's lives hung in the balance of his decisions, and she'd always marveled at the way in which he handled his job. He was the essence of a man who took his responsibilities seriously. Yet, this time was different. She knew that, in addition to his concern, he was weighed down by something else. Her husband and Philip Stevens had known and respected each other for more than thirty years. Their friendship had started during World War II, when Herb, then a lieutenant commander, had been the Navy's liaison with the shipbuilding division of the Stevens Corporation.

Admiral Corrigan took the shaving kit from his wife, gave her a kiss on the cheek, and left the bedroom. Any thought of a fishing vacation was gone from his mind. One thing preoccupied him: he had to locate and rescue the missing Stevens 747.

The weather seemed to be getting worse, and inside the cockpit of the 747, Banker grew uncomfortable as the bumpiness of the ride increased. Chambers had again switched the radio to the search-and-rescue frequency.

The cross talk between the planes involved in the search filled the cockpit.

"Search Base, this is Search Two. Proceeding to Sector Charlie. Over."

"Search Two. This is Search Base. Message received. Out."

Banker knew that he was hearing the communication to the Navy planes that were searching for them. He felt a little concerned. He mentioned this to Chambers. Chambers laughed.

"Those planes are heading to the place we're supposed to be. Don't forget, we're heading away from that area at six hundred miles an hour."

Banker looked at Chambers steadily. "No chance a search plane could come across us by accident?"

Chambers shrugged. "We're already two hundred miles off course. There isn't a chance in hell anyone could spot us."

Banker felt angry. Somehow, he felt that Chambers was laughing at him, and Banker didn't like to be laughed at or thought ignorant. But if he were going to deal with Chambers, the time for that certainly wasn't now. Banker looked at his watch. "I better go help Wilson," he said, and got up out of the pilot's seat.

As he exited the cockpit and walked down the stairs to the main lounge, the anger in him grew. He really didn't like Chambers. He hadn't liked Chambers' continuing fears about the operation, and he didn't like the fact that Chambers was an amateur, a man who, after the split, might accidentally get too talkative. And, Banker knew, a talkative partner could be a deadly thing. He shifted the gun tucked into his belt. After this flight, it didn't really matter at all what happened to Chambers.

In the main lounge, Banker noticed that many of the guests were fitfully stirring. He could even hear several of the passengers moaning. Banker was glad that they were only fifteen minutes away from St. George Island and the landing. The guests would be awake soon.

97

Banker started down the stairs to the forward cargo hold. Yes, after the landing, they didn't need Chambers for a thing. In fact, at that point, considering the division of the money, you could say that Chambers was just another obstacle. Banker smiled to himself. It was certainly an interesting line of thought.

Banker entered the forward cargo hold. He saw that Wilson was hard at work, stacking paintings in front of the cargo-hold loading door. Banker took off his steward's coat, opened an aluminum cargo container, and began to help Wilson. Banker knew they'd not be able to remove the huge cargo containers from the plane. Instead of even trying, he'd planned from the start to have as many pictures as possible piled up and ready to be removed from the 747. That way, they'd lose as little time as possible, once they were on the island. Yes, he thought, I've planned everything down to the minute. Banker was satisfied. They were reaching the end of a long, intricate plan, a plan that he alone had originated. It was going to succeed. Nothing could go wrong now.

The first thing that Admiral Herb Corrigan did when he arrived at the Navy Tactical Coordination Center was to instruct an aide to locate Philip Stevens and get him on the telephone. The aide hurried away, and Corrigan headed for the coordination center's situation room.

He scarcely noticed the sailors who snapped to attention as he hurried down the long corridor toward the situation room. His years of experience as commanding officer were already taking over. He was deep in concentration, sorting out the various rescue possibilities that existed.

Corrigan entered the situation room. He could tell from the well-ordered activity and the sense of tension in the air that the search effort was already well under way. The situation room would be the base of operations for the entire search effort. The room was almost the size of a basketball court, and was very tall. This made it possible for situation maps to be flashed on huge screens that lined the walls. Corrigan's eyes flicked from one screen to another. He was able to quickly assess the status of the search effort from what he saw. One screen showed him the current locations of all rescue planes on this mission. Another showed the areas that had already been searched. A third showed the location of Navy and Coast Guard ships that were within fifty miles of the area where the 747 had disappeared. A fourth showed the approximate locations of commercial ships that were in the area. And a fifth showed the recent weather conditions that were prevailing. The floor of the room contained lines of radarscopes that were being operated by sailors. The equipment that filled this room represented an investment of many millions of dollars, and Corrigan was justifiably proud that this investment was willingly made so that aircraft and ships could move safely through America's coastal waters.

The cross talk between the Navy and Coast Guard search planes was being monitored. The babble of voices from many radio channels being monitored at once filled the room. To an outsider it would have seemed like a babble of static mixed with some foreign language that sounded almost like English.

"Search Base, this is Red Seven. No contact in Area Michael. Moving to Area Norman."

But to the personnel in the situation room of the coordination center, the language that was being spoken was an easily understood but precise shorthand that let them know, in an instant, the minute-by-minute progress of the operation and the whereabouts of the search planes.

Admiral Corrigan was immediately spotted by his second-in-command, Commander Laurence Reed. The two men had worked together for nearly ten years, and they spent no time in greetings. Reed instantly handed Corrigan a summary of the operation to that moment, then led Corrigan over to the planning console.

The planning console was an area that was in the middle of the room. It contained repeater screens that provided instant access to information as it came in. It also contained a large map table illuminated by a glaring overhead spotlight. On the table was a complete navigational chart of the area in which the Stevens 747 was presumed to have disappeared. The chart was demarcated into squares. Each square represented twenty square miles of ocean. This chart was the basis of a standard rescue operation known as a "square search." It was a method of operation that was both logical and efficient. All ships and planes that were engaged in the search were divided into different groups. The group commanders would assign one aircraft, or one ship, to search one twenty-mile square of ocean. The search units worked outward, from the point where the 747 was last heard from. The disadvantage of this method was that it was slow. But it was exhaustive; if the 747 were out there, this method was the surest way of finding it.

Corrigan leaned his arms against the table and studied the chart. Only a few of the squares on the map had been marked off with grease pencil. That designated an area that had been searched already. Corrigan, as he always did, wished that the search could proceed much more quickly. Until most of the squares on the map were crossed off, the search would be like looking for a needle in a haystack. Actually, he thought, in comparative terms, it might be easier to find a needle in a haystack than it was to find one lost plane in the enormity of the ocean. Yet, it was a miracle that he knew they pulled off daily. Their record of recoveries was the best in the Navy.

"Any progress?" said Corrigan.

Reed shook his head. "Negative, sir. We've got twenty S-3 search jets out there. Also, there's a Coast Guard cutter in the area. But there's been no sighting of a plane or debris."

Corrigan nodded and moved to the weather printout machine. This was one of the latest developments in weather technology. Its information came directly via a satellite that tracked the entire Atlantic seacoast and continuously relayed its information to the Cape

Kennedy tracking station. From there the information was relayed to Jacksonville, where by computer it was transferred to the printout machine. The machine disgorged a long roll of paper on which was printed a series of maps of the Atlantic coast and ocean. Overlaid on the map were different swirls of colors, which represented the weather fronts for the different areas of the entire sector. Through the use of these maps it was possible for the staff of the coordination center to constantly know the weather conditions for the entire search site.

Corrigan studied the maps, and with his finger traced a pattern that indicated that a weather front was moving into the northern sector. He knew that a great deal of fog would accompany that weather front. He turned to Reed. "The *Galway* is in the area. Isn't it?"

"Yes, sir," Reed said.

The big aircraft carrier was exactly what they needed. "We're going to have to make this fast," Corrigan said. "This weather front's going to bring zero visibility with it. Let's get fifteen more S-3 jets into the air. We've got to get as much use out of whatever visibility we have left, as we can. Also, you better get CINCLANT fleet on the phone. When that fog socks in, we'll have to convert to a sea search. I want to get every available ship I can into that area."

"Yes, sir," Reed said. He turned and hurried to carry out the admiral's orders.

A sailor approached Corrigan. "Sir," he said. "We've located Mr. Stevens for you. He's on the phone, line nine."

Corrigan nodded and picked up the phone. He had long experience in dealing with the relatives of military personnel who had been lost at sea. But he didn't quite know how he was going to handle this one. Not only was Stevens his friend, but Corrigan had learned from the flight manifest that Stevens' daughter and grandson were on board the plane. Abruptly he pushed the button that connected him to line nine.

As it turned out, it was less difficult than Corrigan had expected. Although Philip Stevens was taking it hard, he was keeping himself well under control. Corrigan tried to be optimistic with him, but Stevens cut him short.

"Look, Herb. The situation's very grave. There's no getting around it. But I know that if you're heading this operation, everything that possibly can be done to find that plane will be done."

Corrigan was moved by Stevens' courage. He reacted spontaneously. "Phil, why don't you join us here in Jacksonville? We're monitoring the Coast Guard's search as well as our own. You can get here by plane in less than an hour. If anything's going to break, it'll come through here first."

Stevens' sober tone brightened. "Thanks, Herb. I'm on my way."

"I'll have them clear you for landing at the military field," Corrigan said.

After saying good-bye, Corrigan hung up the phone, stood there for a moment, then took out a cigarette and lit it. He listened to the tinny voices that came from the rescue channels. Those strange voices seemed transmitted from the other side of the world. They were one of the few links that the center had with the vast homeless ocean out there. Corrigan suddenly felt immense compassion for the tremendous anxiety that Philip Stevens must feel. Best not to think of that. He took a deep drag on his cigarette and watched his men at their jobs, intently keeping alert over their radarscopes, listening carefully to the radioed search reports, updating their weather data as they tried to stay one jump ahead of the dangerous ocean. They were damn good men, Corrigan thought to himself, and that's what counted. He saw Commander Reed approaching him. He knew that Reed would tell him that they could now begin coordination with CINCLANT fleet's operations. Stubbing out his cigarette, Corrigan prepared himself. It was going to be a very long night.

Chambers maintained a careful watch on the altimeter as the plane flew on. He easily maintained a distance of three hundred feet from the water. For a long time, a foggy mist had been building. Now it had grown so thick that he was flying on instruments. Occasionally the plane would break through the fog bank into a clear area. Then, for a few moments, Chambers would catch a glimpse of the water below, only to have that view snatched away again by the all-enveloping fog.

As Chambers flew the plane, he felt a certain amount of relief. Soon they'd be at the island. There'd be sufficient time for them to unload, then transfer the art goods to the plane that would be waiting for them there. Hopefully, by this time tomorrow he'd be in Rio with a new identity and a fortune. Still, there was a large quantity of sadness mixed with his relief. He'd never thought of himself as a criminal before. In fact, he'd never even thought of himself as a bad man. Now there was incontrovertible evidence that he was both. Yet, what choice had he ever had? What he had always thought himself to be was weak. And, he thought, there was certainly enough evidence of that. For instance, the compulsions that drove him to Las Vegas, where he had indulged in week-long gambling forays that had eventually drained his savings. He had tried to get even again by betting still greater sums. He soon had markers out to a number of unsavory characters, and instead of getting rid of his debts, he found he was in deeper than he had been before. He was two hundred and fifty thousand dollars in debt, and there was no solution in sight.

It was at that moment that Banker had suddenly appeared. Banker had been looking for a pilot with his kind of problems, and it was Banker's influence that had allowed him to have so much credit with the bookies. Then he made Chambers this offer: cooperate, and have no debts, and a fortune besides. Refuse, and Banker would allow the gambling syndicate to collect its debts immediately—in blood. There had really been no choice.

It was strange, Chambers thought. He knew he would soon be a rich man. Yet, he looked on his total life as one of failure and waste. This entire line of thought was dragging down his spirits. He abruptly pushed all this to the back of his mind and brought his full attention to flying the aircraft. The fog was beginning to clear again, and he looked down and could see the water speeding by below. Ahead of him he could see the fog breaking up, and for a moment he thought he saw a vague outline of something. Chambers strained his eyes to see, but soon the fog gathered around the 747, and he decided that what he had seen was just a shadow in the fog.

As it turned out, he was wrong—horribly and irrevocably wrong.

Suddenly, directly in Chambers' line of vision, there was a green glow. It seemed to be coming directly toward the windscreen of the plane. Chambers instantly recognized it for what it was. The 747 was heading directly toward the marker light of a deep-sea oil-drilling rig.

Like all commercial pilots, Chambers had been trained to react instantly in an emergency situation. He immediately pulled back on the wheel and increased the thrust of the jets. He was trying desperately to pull the nose of the plane up, to gain enough altitude so that the 747 would miss the certain disaster that would result from a head-on collision with the steel oil-drilling derrick.

He almost made it. As the nose of the plane rose, there was a sudden jolt, followed by the scream of metal, and Chambers knew that the wing of the 747 had struck the top of the tower. Red lights began blinking on the panel, and as he struggled to regain control of the plane, a part of his mind noted what was going on and objectively figured out the chances for survival. The plane bucked and reared. That, Chambers knew, meant that control cables had been destroyed in the starboard wing. A reddish glow filled the cockpit, and he knew that at least one of the starboard engines was on fire. Calmly, Chambers hit the number four engine fire-bottle controls. Then he applied more thrust to the port-side engines, and continued to gain altitude. Four, five, six hundred feet. Then the plane shook, and there was the sound of an explosion. Number three starboard-side engine had exploded, probably because it had ingested some debris from the other disabled engines. Quickly Chambers feathered the two starboard engines. As his hands raced from control to control, there was a part of his mind that remained strangely objective and detached. That part of his mind noted the disintegration of the 747's systems. It watched Chambers' efforts to control the plane failing, and maintained the cold detachment of the surgeon who knows an operation is going badly but who coolly files this information away for future reference. What was happening, Chambers thought, was very much like the disasters that had been programmed into the training simulators he had used when he was learning his trade. Only, now it was for real.

When the impact with the oil derrick occurred, Banker and Wilson were in the forward cargo hold removing paintings from the aluminum cargo containers and stacking them near the cargo hold's loading door. The cargo hold was much closer to the point of impact than any other area of the 747. Consequently, the force of the impact was much greater there. At the moment of impact, Wilson was very lucky. He was standing near the loading door and was able to grab a structural girder for support. Banker, however, had no such advantage. He had been standing near an open cargo container and had nothing to grab on to. As a result, when the impact came, he was thrown across the hold, and when he landed against the bulkhead, his head impacted against the wall with a sickening thud.

For a moment Wilson had clung to the structural girder in unmoving terror. Gradually, however, he came to his senses and realized that he had to get out of that cargo hold. As the floor vibrated and moved underfoot, Wilson carefully crossed the cargo compartment and knelt by Banker. Banker was groggy and couldn't get to his feet. Wilson tried futilely to help him. Then, when the shaking of the plane became more pronounced, he again panicked. Abandoning Banker, Wilson hurried out of the cargo hold as fast as his feet could carry him. Weakly,

Banker called after him. But it did no good. Wilson disappeared through the door of the hold, and the door swung shut of its own weight, its safety catches locking it into place.

The shaking of the plane had become so violent that Wilson had trouble keeping his footing on the stairs that led up to the main lounge. Holding on to the railing with all his strength, he literally had to grapple to drag himself up the stairs.

The main lounge was lit by a pink glow that told him the engines on the starboard side were on fire. The lurching of the plane made walking difficult, and as he made his way to the stairs that led to the flight deck, he used various pieces of furniture to steady himself. Wilson saw that many of the guests were coming to groggy consciousness. The violent shaking of the plane was, no doubt, bringing them to. The air was filled with groans and screams as the passengers came to full, fearful awareness.

Wilson struggled up the stairs to the flight deck. Opening the cockpit door, he moved inside. He saw that the instrument panels were a myriad of blinking red lights and that Chambers was struggling vainly to control the plane. But, worse than that, Wilson saw that the water was screaming up at them and that they were clearly going to crash.

Pilot Don Gallagher
(Jack Lemmon)

Karen Wallace
(Lee Grant)

Eve Clayton
(Brenda Vaccaro)

Emily Livingston
(Olivia De Havilland)

Nicholas St. Downs III
(Joseph Cotten)

Stan Buchek
(Darren McGavin)

Martin Wallace
(Christopher Lee)

Philip Stevens
(James Stewart)

Patroni
(George Kennedy)

Millionaire philanthropist Philip Stevens
(James Stewart)

Nicholas St. Downs III *(Joseph Cotten)* and Emily Livingston *(Olivia De Havilland)* portray old flames who are reunited as they journey toward an art museum opening aboard a private 747 destined to meet disaster in the skies.

A tipsy Karen Wallace *(Lee Grant)* flirts with her husband's business associate *(Gil Gerard)*—who also happens to be her former lover. *Below* oceanographer Martin Wallace *(Christopher Lee)* confers with his associate *(Gil Gerard)* as they fly towards a rendezvous with disaster.

Executive assistant Eve Clayton *(Brenda Vaccaro)* and jet pilot Don Gallagher *(Jack Lemmon)* share a romantic interlude before mid-air disaster strikes.

Eve Clayton *(Brenda Vaccaro)* struggles to calm panicky Karen Wallace *(Lee Grant)* after an air disaster hurls their jumbo jet into the waters of the Bermuda Triangle.

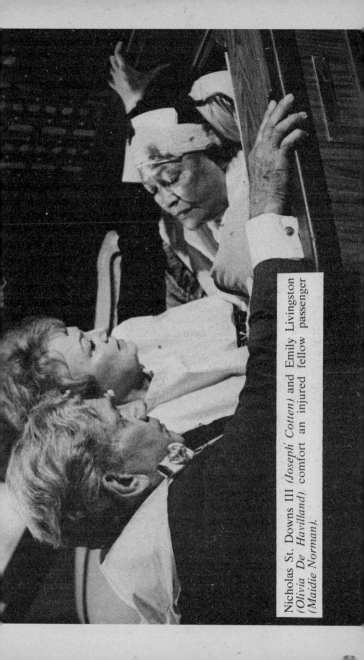

Nicholas St. Downs III (*Joseph Cotten*) and Emily Livingston (*Olivia De Havilland*) comfort an injured fellow passenger (*Maidie Norman*).

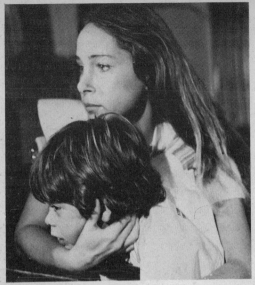

Lisa Stevens *(Pamela Bellwood)* holds her son *(Anthony Battaglia)* as they wait to be rescued. *Below* pilot Don Gallagher *(Jack Lemmon)* and aircraft designer Stan Buchek *(Darren McGavin)* study the plans of their downed jumbo jet before they attempt to raise it from the ocean floor.

Philip Stevens *(James Stewart)* joins in the attempt to rescue the passengers aboard his downed private jet.

Eddy, the bartender (Robert Hooks), Eve Clayton (Brenda Vaccaro), Nicholas St. Downs III (Joseph Cotten), and Emily Livingston (Olivia De Havilland) are caught in the deluge as their disaster-stricken jumbo jet floods in the perilous waters of the Bermuda Triangle.

Don Gallagher *(Jack Lemmon)* and Eve Clayton *(Brenda Vaccaro)* struggle to escape the flood of seawater pouring into their downed 747.

Martin Wallace *(Christopher Lee)* prepares to risk his life to save the trapped passengers.

Millionaire Philip Stevens *(James Stewart)* embraces his daughter *(Pamela Bellwood)* and grandson *(Anthony Battaglia)* after their dramatic rescue from the downed 747.

11

Gallagher didn't know how long he had been fighting for consciousness, but it seemed that he had been swimming through an eternity of blackness. Minutes ago he had fought the waves of nausea that shook him and forced himself to a sitting position. Now he felt his strength returning and he forced himself to his feet. The steep angle of the plane and its violent motion had awakened the survival instinct in him. He didn't know what had happened, but a part of him screamed that he had to help himself and help his passengers. Staggering, Gallagher made his way out of the bedroom and into the corridor. The pink glow of the burning engines filled the corridor and intensified his desire to get to the passengers. Moving as quickly as he could, he made his way to the main lounge.

As Gallagher entered the main lounge, a sight of terrible chaos greeted him. Groans and screams filled the air. He saw that Mrs. Stern was trying to get up and was screaming for her daughter. The little girl was nowhere to be seen. A sudden lurch of the plane threw the woman to the floor. As Gallagher moved toward the center of the lounge, he felt a pair of hands grab him. It was Karen Wallace. Hysterical, she grasped him desperately, screaming. He grasped her shoulders and forced her down, into the arms of Frank Powers and her husband. He shouted to the passengers, trying to get their attention.

"Face the rear of the plane. Get your backs against anything solid!"

Some passengers heard him and complied. Gallagher moved toward others, forcing them down on the floor, grabbing pillows from chairs and sofas, and piling the pillows around the guests. As Gallagher moved among the guests, the panic began to subside, and they began to follow his directions.

Gallagher saw that St. Downs had helped Emily Livingston to the bulkhead. He had placed his back to the wall and pulled Emily close to him. Gallagher passed them and ran to Jane Stern, who was screaming for her daughter. He forced her to move between two couches. Looking up, Gallagher saw that Buchek was approaching, with Benjy under one arm. Buchek passed the boy to Gallagher, and Gallagher placed the child in Mrs. Stern's arms.

"Stay here. We'll find your daughter."

Mrs. Stern nodded and held the little boy closely to her.

Gallagher headed toward the forward part of the lounge. He knew that he had to get to the cockpit. As he moved toward the stairs that led to the flight deck, he saw Buchek pick up Jane Stern's daughter, then head toward the woman.

The angle of the plane's descent was becoming steeper. As the angle increased, food, glasses, dishes, and any other loose object began to slide forward in the lounge.

Gallagher reached the stairs that led to the flight deck, but by this time the angle of the plane was so steep that all he could do was hang on to the railing. The shaking and bucking of the plane increased, and as Gallagher clung to the railing, he could think of only one thing: Where was Eve?

Chambers desperately tried to level out the plane. If he could make the 747 hit the water belly-first, instead of nose-first, they might all have some chance of survival. He tried to lower the flaps and thereby slow down their airspeed, but by this time most of the plane's systems were no longer functional. The plane bucked and reared as it went down. Desperately Chambers continued to pull back on the wheel with all his strength. He had almost leveled out the 747 when the plane's belly hit the water with tremendous force. The shock was like being caught in the middle of a tremendous explosion.

In the main lounge, the effect of the crash was instantaneous. Ceiling panels and light fixtures tore loose. Sections of rosewood wall paneling were sent sailing through the lounge. Tables, chairs, and sofas went careening through the room, in some cases seriously injuring passengers. Liquor bottles, food, glasses, metal trays—anything that wasn't nailed down went flying through the air.

Gallagher was caught on the stairs leading up to the cockpit. He was slammed over the railing and onto the floor of the main lounge by the force of the crash. Then he was suddenly showered with broken glass from the bar. The sheer jolting noise of the crash seemed deafening. Gallagher saw a blur of motion pass by. When he heard the explosion of glass and the scream of agony, he knew that what he had seen was a uniformed steward, tossed like a projectile, through the screen of the wall-size television unit.

The explosive force generated by the impact grasped the passengers like some malevolent invisible hand. Steve Burroughs was thrown against the side of the plane, behind the piano bar. The piano was torn loose from its moorings and was savagely propelled toward him. It tore into his body at chest level. There was agony as he felt the crack of breaking ribs. Suddenly, pain swept him, and he felt as if a knife had been stabbed into his abdomen. He let out a shriek of pain.

Steve's scream was buried amid the welter of sounds that seemed to swell up like a geyser—the tearing and twisting of metal, the sounds of human fear and pain.

The plane shuddered and rolled toward one side. Gallagher grabbed a partition to steady himself and, to his horror, saw a guest rushing toward the tottering wall-size television. The television unit teetered, then, in an avalanche of metal and broken glass, fell, striking the guest on the head, then pinning him to the floor.

Then, just as suddenly as it had happened, the force of initial impact was over.

Miraculously, no water seemed to have penetrated the passenger area of the plane. Yet, the plane moved and rolled atop the rough sea. The air was filled with screams, and Gallagher could see the passengers holding on to furniture, clutching each other, and holding on to whatever support they could find. They were terrified, not knowing what was going to happen next, or if they were to live or die.

Gallagher knew that they didn't dare open the exit door until the passengers were organized and ready to get out of the plane quickly. Once the pressure seal was broken on that exit door, the plane could sink like a stone in very few minutes. Yet, as he looked around him, Gallagher wondered how he could quickly make order out of the chaos that surrounded him. Some people were trapped by debris, many were injured seriously, others were scattered throughout the rest of the huge plane. Gallagher would get them ready, but deep inside, he knew there wasn't enough time.

Gallagher heard Mrs. Stern scream her daughter's name. Then Gallagher saw why.

The massive oak bar had toppled. The little girl had somehow become wedged between the bar and the wall of the plane. She was sobbing loudly. Near her, Buchek lay, his arm pinned underneath the bar. Obviously he had been caught while he was trying to save the girl. Buchek's face was a grimace of pain, and Gallagher could see that his arm was probably broken. He leaped to his feet and ran to the bar. He and Mrs. Stern tried desperately to lift the bar before the motion of the plane slid it any farther. If they failed, it was possible that Bonnie would be crushed. From out of nowhere, Nicholas St. Downs was beside Gallagher, putting his strength against the weight of the bar. Somehow they lifted it enough so that Jane Stern could kneel down and gently draw Bonnie to safety. She held the sobbing child in her arms as Buchek carefully slid his injured arm out from under the bar. Gallagher and St. Downs let the bar fall back to the floor. Gallagher knelt beside the grimacing Buchek and helped him to his feet. Buchek was wobbly, but he made it. His arm hung limply at his side. Gallagher touched the arm, and Buchek winced. It was clearly a bad fracture.

"Help the others," Buchek said. "They're in worse shape than I am."

Gallagher nodded, then began organizing passengers. He ordered the fit to help carry the injured to the area near one of the exit doors. Then he sent several passengers to check out the rear and forward portions of the plane to seek out the injured. Gallagher paused at the piano and helped several men pull it away from Steve. Julie Denton rushed past him. She went to Steve, who was barely conscious. There was a stunned expression on his face. He held his hand across his abdomen, and a slight moan issued from his lips. Gently, Julie took him into her arms and held him close.

As Gallagher smoothly organized the guests, he passed Emily Livingston, who was cradling Dorothy in her arms. Dorothy had livid bruises on her face, and blood was issuing from a serious scalp laceration. Emily pressed a handkerchief over the flow of blood. As Gallagher worked, swiftly and surely, he felt angry at the senseless tragedy that had befallen them. But there was no time to think of that now. He knew that they had only minutes to save themselves, possibly less.

Minutes before the plane crashed, Banker was still on the floor of the forward cargo compartment, where Wilson had left him. He had gradually returned to consciousness after cracking his head against the bulkhead. There was a sharp pain near his ear, and he had trouble focusing his eyes.

Banker was completely unprepared when the giant plane hit the water. Worse, the forward cargo hold was the major point of impact when the plane crashed.

The plane hit, and Banker was flung against the bulkhead. He saw the huge aluminum cargo containers propelled across the cargo compartment. Although each weighed more than a thousand pounds, they moved across the cargo hold like matchsticks. One of the cargo containers spun toward the side of the plane. It hit with incredible force, and Banker watched with horror as a gaping hole began to open. Abruptly, a roaring cascade of thousands of gallons of seawater was spilling into the cargo hold. The body of the plane moved again, sending the cargo container rolling back toward him in the cargo hold. He tried to move away, but it all was happening too quickly. He felt a screaming pain as the cargo container pressed against him, pinning him to the bulkhead. He shrieked in agony as the pressure against his body became unbearable. He lay behind the container, pinioned. It felt as if he were nailed to the wall. The seawater that filled the cargo hold was shocking in its coldness. Banker, who had never before felt helpless, began to sob. The water rose quickly, and suddenly Banker began to swallow the salty brine. He choked and tried to breathe in air, but there was no air left to breathe. His screams stopped, and now the only sound left was that of the ocean as it filled the cargo hold to the ceiling.

Outside, illuminated by the moon, the giant 747 slowly began to list to one side. The seawater that had filled the cargo hold had tipped the great plane's balance, and what buoyancy the plane had possessed was destroyed. Slowly the plane rolled and sank into the ocean. It was headed straight to the bottom of the murky water.

12

Martin Wallace and Frank Powers pulled desperately at the fallen wall-size television set. During the crash, it had landed on a man, and the two were struggling to free him. Powers called out for help, and they were joined by two other guests. Their combined efforts yielded results. With great effort they raised the TV enough to free the man underneath. Carefully they slid him out from under the set, then lowered the television back to the floor. The man was covered with blood, and it was instantly apparent that the set's heavy mahogany case had crushed his rib cage. Martin Wallace bent over the man, listening for a heartbeat, but it was clear that he had probably died instantly. As Wallace was getting up, he heard a voice that was unmistakably his wife's.

"Oh, my God. Look!"

The voice was filled with such incredible horror that Wallace and all who were within earshot turned toward Karen, who was pointing toward the windows of the plane.

The water outside the plane was quickly rising above the windows.

There was a moment of hush as the guests took in what was happening. Then, screams of horror as the floor of the plane began to shift under their feet. The debris and furniture began to shift again, and the guests began falling as they grabbed for handholds and footholds. The angle of the floor increased, and Martin Wallace felt himself sliding toward the back of the main lounge. He grabbed a couch, but quickly that began sliding too. Once again there was panic and utter confusion. Suddenly the lights began to flicker. Abruptly they went out. As the plane continued to drop toward the bottom of the ocean, Martin Wallace thought it was like one of those horrible dreams when he felt he was falling into endless darkness. Except that this, he knew, was no dream.

Buchek was holding on to the toppled bar. As the plane sank, Buchek also felt raw terror. But, at the same time, his engineer's mind was making all sorts of calculations. He knew that the weight of water in the lower portions of the plane must be dragging them inexorably downward to the bottom of the ocean. Yet, there must be no leaks in the passenger areas. If there had been, flooding would have begun immediately, and the fuselage would most likely have begun to break up as soon as the plane began to sink. But, he thought, how well could the fuselage withstand contact with the bottom of the ocean?

The screams and cries of the guests were suddenly drowned out by a huge noise and a bone-crushing jar. The 747 had struck the bottom of the ocean. The plane settled, with a groan of protesting metal. Then, miraculously, there was silence, penetrated only by the sobs that came from several of the passengers. It was pitch-black inside the airliner.

Buchek reached inside his pocket and took out a tiny penlight. He thanked God for whatever it was that had reminded him to place it in his pocket that morning. He flicked on the light and moved it around the main lounge, picking up the terrified faces of the other passengers.

"Now, listen to me," he said. "There's emergency battery lighting for this area. I want everyone to sit tight while I turn it on."

Carefully Buchek picked his way through the debris and headed toward the corridor that led to the rear of the plane. He noticed the angle of the floor and realized that the plane was resting at quite a steep angle. Finally he reached the rear of the main lounge and stepped into the corridor. There he found what he was looking for—a circuit-breaker box that contained the switches for the emergency lighting. He knew that the batteries that powered these lights were in a special compartment in the rear of the plane. They would function only if they hadn't gotten wet. Wishing himself luck, he flicked the switches that controlled the emergency lights. The lights flickered, but came on and began illuminating the main lounge with small pools of light. Buchek breathed a sigh of relief. He knew he'd immediately have to begin an inspection of the passenger areas in order to make an evaluation of the structural damage to the plane. He didn't know how long the fuselage would hold the water outside. But finding out was vitally important to the survival of everyone.

Karen Wallace was terrified. As the lights came on, her terror increased instead of abated. Around her was the devastating evidence of the crash. Debris was everywhere. The groans and cries of the injured filled her ears. All she could think of was getting out of the plane. The water that surrounded her felt incredibly oppressive. Looking around the main lounge, her eyes came to rest on the life-preserver bin. She got up, and without saying anything, hurried to the bin and extracted a life jacket. She tried to put it on, but in her panic tangled the straps. Discarding the jacket, she took another from the bin and began trying to put it on. Another guest saw her at the bin and rose to join her. Others followed, and soon there was a pushing, shoving group of guests fighting to remove the life jackets from the bin and put them on.

Suddenly Gallagher waded into the midst of the guests, pushing them and shoving them aside. Angrily he shouted at them. "Forget those life jackets. We can't open the doors without flooding the plane!"

Gallagher was suddenly bombarded with anxious questions.

"We've got to get out, we'll drown in here."

"Have you radioed for help?"

"What are we going to do? We'll run out of air before they find us."

Gallagher quickly answered them as well as he was

able. He knew he had to restore some sense of security to the guests or the panic would lead to their destruction as surely as the water outside would. He explained that the pressurization of the passenger areas was obviously holding. Otherwise, the main lounge would already be flooded. As long as the pressurization held, they'd be relatively safe. He let them know that the radio wouldn't work underwater, but their flight had been tracked on radar, and help was no doubt rushing to them. Finally he felt that their immediate panic was under control. He knew what had to be done to keep it under control.

"Now, listen to me," he said. "A lot of people are hurt, and our first duty is to help them." Gallagher motioned to Julie. "Julie, you help the stewardesses. Bring blankets, sheets, pillows, anything we can use to help make the injured more comfortable."

Anxiety-stricken, Julie shook her head. "Steve's hurt bad. You've got to help him."

Gallagher nodded. "We'll see that everyone who needs help gets it. But we need those blankets and sheets. Get moving."

Her lips tight, Julie nodded. She and the stewardesses headed to the corridor that led to the rear of the plane.

Gallagher spotted Herb Williams, who was finishing the bandage on a man's arm. "Are you a doctor?" he asked.

Williams nodded as he completed his work.

"Good," Gallagher said. "There's a child by the bar. She's seriously injured. Help her, then take a look at Steve."

Williams got up and headed toward the toppled bar.

Gallagher pointed to two other men. "You two. Go with him and help." The men nodded, and quickly followed the doctor. Gallagher started to move through the debris, then quickly dropped to his knees as he saw a man whose blood pulsed out of a severed artery in his arm. The man sat motionless, in shock. With both hands Gallagher grabbed the arm and squeezed with all his force, slowing the flood of blood. He shouted, "Get a tourniquet on this man's arm. Quick!"

Gallagher looked up. Karen Wallace was standing nearby, a dazed look on her face. Gallagher called to her. "Mrs. Wallace. Give me the belt off your dress. Quick."

Karen looked at him as if she hadn't heard him at all.

"How could you have let this happen to us, Captain? It's all your fault."

Angry, Gallagher looked around. "Goddammit. This man is bleeding to death. Somebody give me a belt!"

Lucas came forward, taking his belt off as he walked. He quickly knelt down and looped the belt around the man's arm. Gallagher grabbed the belt and pulled it tight. The bleeding diminished quickly, then stopped.

Turning the tourniquet over to Lucas, Gallagher got up and headed toward the stairs that led to the flight deck. As he was about to mount the stairs, he spotted Buchek coming out of the forward part of the plane.

"The forward part of the lounge is okay. The structural members seem to be holding," he said.

Gallagher nodded. "Good," he said. "Check the rest of the fuselage, then let me know how long you think it'll hold up."

"Right," Buchek said. He moved closer to Gallagher. "Don, what happened?"

"I don't know," Gallagher replied, "but I'm sure as hell going to find out." With that, Gallagher mounted the stairs that led to the flight deck.

Buchek hurried across the main lounge to the corridor that led to the back of the plane. It was imperative that he check the condition of the fuselage, search for leaks, and determine how long the plane could remain intact underwater. He only hoped that it would be long enough for help to come.

Buchek spotted Nicholas St. Downs. He and Emily Livingston were kneeling beside Dorothy, who was lying on the floor. Emily was cradling her head, which was lacerated and hideously bruised. St. Downs was tying a piece of cloth around Dorothy's leg to stop a deep cut from bleeding.

117

Buchek moved to them as St. Downs finished. "I'm going to need some help," he told St. Downs. "Can you come with me?"

St. Downs turned toward Emily and looked at her with concern.

"Go with him, Nicholas," she said firmly. "I'll take care of Dorothy. Go on, I'll be all right."

He flashed her a quick smile. She was a brave woman. Then he followed Buchek to the corridor that led to the rear portion of the plane.

Some ceiling panels had fallen onto the stairs that led to the flight deck. Gallagher pulled them free, then tossed them over the railing of the stairs into the main lounge. After what seemed like an intolerable delay, he mounted the stairs and climbed to the flight deck. He was about to enter the cockpit when he noticed that the door to the office was ajar. Looking inside, he saw a complete shambles. Ceiling and wall panels littered the floor. The teletype machine had toppled, as had the large mahogany desk. But what made a great surge of relief pass through Gallagher was that he saw Eve through the door. She was on the floor, kneeling and cradling a somewhat dazed Lisa in her arms. Near them, in a pool of his own blood, was Walker, the flight engineer. Gallagher quickly moved to Walker and looked for a pulse.

"He's dead," Eve said, her voice breaking as she spoke. Gallagher rose and crossed to the two women.

Steadying herself, Lisa got up and accepted Gallagher's steadying hand. Collecting herself, she spoke to him.

"Where's Benjy? Is he all right?"

"He's downstairs, Lisa. He's fine. He wasn't injured."

"Thank God," she said, and with a sigh of relief she rushed out of the office and down the stairs to the main lounge.

Alone with Eve, Gallagher moved toward her and took her in his arms. Eve began to sob uncontrollably as he soothed her and stroked her hair.

"Don, what happened? What are we going to do?"

He allowed her to sob for a few moments, then held her tightly at arm's length and spoke. "Listen to me, Eve. There are people below who are seriously injured. We've got to help them."

Eve swallowed hard, then began wiping the tears from her eyes.

"I want to, Don, but I'm so afraid."

Smiling, he wiped away the last of her tears. "Those people need your help, Eve...and so do I."

Eve visibly composed herself. "I'll try..."

Gallagher pulled her to him and held her tight.

"You'll do it. I know you will."

"Okay," said Eve. She gave him a brave smile, then headed down the stairs.

Across the main lounge, Dorothy could see Lisa and Benjy. Lisa was holding the little boy close to her, and Dorothy felt relieved that at least one of the two children on board was safe. Strangely, although she was in great pain, all she could think about was the safety of those children. She tried to raise her head and look for Bonnie. But Emily's hand gently restrained her. She focused on Emily's face and saw the look of deep concern in Emily's eyes.

"Where's the little girl? Is she all right?"

Emily smiled at her and spoke softly. "Now, just lie back and let me take care of you."

Dorothy's hand was reaching for Emily's. Emily took her hand and squeezed it. In spite of the pain, Dorothy tried to smile.

"Emily, I'm supposed to be taking care of you."

Emily smiled warmly at her. "We're all supposed to take care of each other, Dorothy. And that's what we're going to do."

Dorothy's eyes closed as she fell into a troubled sleep. Emily was grateful. She feared that Dorothy's injuries were terribly serious, and knew that the more Dorothy slept, the less pain she'd feel. Silently Emily motioned to

Dr. Williams, who was examining Bonnie Stern near the toppled bar. Williams gestured that he'd be right there.

Mrs. Stern watched with great concern as the doctor carefully checked Bonnie for injuries.

He finished the examination and turned to her. "She's an extremely lucky little girl, Mrs. Stern," he said. "She's suffered some bruised ribs, but she's going to be fine."

Mrs. Stern exhaled a deep breath of relief. It was a miracle that Bonnie wasn't seriously injured. If they could only survive until help came, her daughter might have a chance. She turned to thank the doctor, but before she could say a word, he'd hurried away and had moved across the lounge and begun examining Dorothy.

When Gallagher entered the cockpit, he saw that the copilot, Chambers, was sprawled across the control panel. Near him, Wilson lay on the floor, his head at an odd angle. Gallagher knelt by Wilson and felt for signs of life. Wilson's body was already cold. As he was getting up, Gallagher spotted a gas mask lying next to Wilson. He picked it up and studied it for a moment. It was of military design, and seeing it brought into focus a lot of Gallagher's speculations about what had happened. When he moved to Chambers, all his thoughts were confirmed. He saw that Chambers had a .45 automatic tucked into his belt. Gallagher took the gun from the belt and removed its clip of ammunition. Whatever the motive of the conspiracy had been, Chambers, his copilot, had obviously been deeply involved. Disgusted, Gallagher pulled Chambers back into his seat and looked for signs of life. Chambers' face was bloody, and his breath came in irregular gasps. He was unconscious, but to Gallagher it looked as if the man would live. Angry, Gallagher threw the .45 down on the floor of the cockpit. The stupidity and waste that had resulted from what Chambers had done revolted him.

At that moment Gallagher heard feet coming up the stairs from the main lounge. He looked up and saw Crawford heading toward the cockpit. Crawford eased himself into the cramped space.

"Can I help, Captain?"

Gallagher nodded, then spoke as he angrily tugged at Chambers' unconscious body. "Help me get this bastard into the office. When he comes to, he's got a lot of explaining to do."

Crawford quickly moved to join Gallagher, and together the two men eased Chambers out of his seat.

Nicholas St. Downs accompanied Hank Buchek as he moved slowly through the corridor that led to the rear of the 747. Buchek carefully searched for any leaks around windows or any hairline cracks in the window material. As yet, there were none. But he knew that at any moment he might uncover a leak—or a potential leak—that would put the signature on all their death warrants.

Up ahead, Julie Denton and one of the stewardesses came out of the plane's bedroom. Carrying blankets and sheets in their arms, they hurried past Buchek and St. Downs on their way to the main lounge.

As Buchek ran his hand along the wall, feeling for signs of water behind the paneling, St. Downs tried to open the door to the library. The door was wedged shut. He put his shoulder to the door, gave it a push, and the door popped open.

The once-beautiful library was now a shambles. The panels had been jarred loose from the ceiling by the intensity of the crash, and broken glass from the desk lamps littered the floor. Rare books were strewn everywhere, and the desk had crashed into the rosewood paneling of one wall.

As Buchek and St. Downs entered the room, Buchek knocked his arm against the doorway. He winced in pain. St. Downs saw this and noticed the unnatural angle at which Buchek held his arm.

"That looks bad," he said. "Let me make a sling for it."

"Thanks," Buchek said.

St. Downs removed his tie and approached Buchek. Buchek, with some difficulty, brought his arm up to his chest, and St. Downs slipped the tie around to create a sling. It hurt like hell to move the arm, but Buchek knew that the sling's support would take the weight off the arm and that it would begin to feel better. Buchek stayed still as St. Downs knotted the tie around the back of his neck.

As St. Downs tied the knot, Buchek scanned the far wall of the library. The paneling was hanging loose, and there was something about that that he didn't like.

St. Downs finished his task. "How does that feel?" he asked. "Any better?"

Buchek didn't answer. His mind was already occupied by what he felt might be a big problem. "Give me a hand over here," he said to St. Downs.

He stepped over to the wall. The paneling had exposed the fuselage and the aluminum skin of the plane. With his good hand Buchek grasped some of the paneling. St. Downs helped him, and together the two men pulled the loose paneling off the wall.

There it was. A large, ominous bulge in the skin of the plane. Buchek ran his hand over it. At least it wasn't leaking—yet.

St. Downs turned to Buchek. He could see the look of concern on the man's face.

"What do you think?" he asked Buchek. "Will it hold?"

Buchek shrugged. "This plane is pretty strong. But it was never built to withstand this much outside pressure."

"How long can it hold up?"

"I don't know," Buchek said. "Long enough for the rescue units to get here—I hope."

There was a trace of desperation in Buchek's voice. He pulled his hand back from the fuselage. Christ. There had to be something they could do! Then, slowly, Buchek became aware of a low sound. It was faint but distinct.

It was the sound of a human being—a human being moaning in pain.

Buchek rushed to the door that connected the library with the communications room. With his good hand he tugged the door open.

The communications room was virtually destroyed. The radio-telephone unit had shifted position and toppled over. Beneath it was Eddie, the bartender. His leg, which was soaked in blood, was caught beneath the wreckage. Somehow, upon seeing Buchek, he attempted a grin. His voice hoarse with pain, he managed to say, "Christ, Mr. Buchek, am I glad to see you."

Quickly Buchek stepped through the wreckage and into the small room, followed by St. Downs. Together they managed to shift the metal cabinet off Eddie's leg. Eddie groaned.

When Buchek knelt down beside Eddie, he could see how badly Eddie was hurt. It was a compound fracture, and part of the jagged leg bone had torn through Eddie's pantleg.

St. Downs took a small penknife from his pocket and opened it. He leaned close to Eddie and spoke. "Eddie, your leg's beginning to swell. I want to cut that pantleg loose so it won't constrict the circulation. It's going to hurt."

"Okay." Eddie's voice was a whisper.

Buchek grabbed Eddie's shoulder with his good arm and did his best to hold the man down as St. Downs carefully started cutting through the trouser fabric. The pain was so great that Buchek thought Eddie's screams must have carried to the main lounge. Finally St. Downs was done. Sweat was oozing from Eddie's face, and his breathing was labored. "Oh, Jesus," he said. "Oh, Jesus Christ . . ."

Buchek looked down at the leg. It was an ugly sight. With the pantleg ripped off and the flesh exposed, the full extent of Eddie's injuries could be seen. The bone had indeed pierced the skin. Luckily, no artery had been severed. Buchek knew that if that had happened, Eddie wouldn't be alive now. However, it was still a dangerous injury, and one that had to be dealt with by a professional.

"Try to lie as still as you can, Eddie," Buchek said to him. "We'll get someone who can take care of that."

Eddie just nodded, exhausted.

Buchek put a hand on St. Downs's shoulder. "You stay here. I'll get Dr. Williams." Buchek hurriedly got to his feet and left the small room.

The men had placed Chambers on the couch in the

upstairs office. He was still unconscious, and Dr. Williams knelt beside him, examining his pupil dilation with a pocket flashlight. Gallagher and Ralph Crawford stood beside the doctor. Gallagher waited impatiently for the completion of the examination. Chambers had information that he needed. Until he knew where they had gone down, he couldn't estimate when he might expect the rescue units to arrive.

Williams flicked off the flashlight and stood up. "His pupil dilation's fine. It's probably a concussion. He should come around."

"When?" said Gallagher.

"That's hard to tell, Captain. Soon . . . perhaps."

Gallagher nodded. It was one more uncertainty in a tangle of uncertainties. He turned to Crawford. "Stay here and keep watch over the copilot. Let me know the minute he regains consciousness."

"Right."

There was work to do for both Gallagher and Dr. Williams, and they quickly left the office and headed down the stairs.

It was calmer now in the main lounge. As Gallagher descended the stairs, he saw that the passengers had gathered together into small groups. They were tending to the injured and trying to keep each other's spirits up. Gallagher saw Buchek make his way through the passengers and debris and hurry toward him. He could tell from the grim line of the man's mouth that Buchek's assessment of the plane's situation was pessimistic. Buchek put his arm around Gallagher's shoulder, and in a quiet voice, to avoid alarming the passengers, filled Gallagher in on the condition of the plane. The fuselage was in very poor condition. Buchek hoped that they could hold out, but leaking could start at any time.

Buchek turned to Dr. Williams. "We've got a man in the communications room who's in pretty bad shape. He's got a fracture, and the bone's sticking through his leg."

Dr. Williams shook his head. "That sounds nasty. I'll get right on it." He hurried away from Gallagher and

Buchek, leaving them to discuss the stresses on the fuselage and the necessity of an inspection of the lower parts of the plane.

As Dr. Williams hurried through the main lounge, he calculated what he'd need. This was going to be a tough one. There was the setting of the leg to do, and for that he'd need someone to hold the man down. It would be horribly painful. Williams stopped at the toppled bar and began rummaging through the wreckage. He found a bottle of bourbon that, miraculously, hadn't been broken in the crash. That would be some help to the poor bastard, he thought.

Williams looked around the main lounge and spotted Martin Wallace and his wife, Karen. Wallace was holding his wife, who was uninjured but seemed very distraught. Williams approached them. "I'm going to need help," he told Martin. "Will you come with me?"

Karen Wallace seemed to cling closer to her husband. Martin looked at her, then made a hard decision. "Yes," he said. "Of course."

"Good," Dr. Williams said. "I'll be in the rear of the plane. In the communications room. Do you know where that is?"

"Yes." Dr. Williams hurried off.

Martin Wallace could feel how hard his wife's hand was gripping his. He knew it was motivated as much by anger as by fear.

Her voice was intense. "Don't leave me. Don't leave me alone."

He knew that reasoning with her would do no good. Yet, he knew that he couldn't keep from trying. There had to be some time when she would see that there were other people in the world. People who had needs, just as she did. He looked down at her, at the frightened eyes and the clenched teeth. Her almost totally animal reaction to their predicament shocked him.

Softly he said, "Karen, there are injured people here who need help."

Her nails dug into him. "You're my husband. You're

125

supposed to take care of *me*. What's going to happen to me?"

"Karen..." He really didn't know what to say to her. "Stay here!"

Martin reached up and pulled Karen's arms away from his shoulders. "I'm sorry, Karen, I have to join the doctor." He tried to take her hand, a conciliatory move, but she pulled away. Suddenly her mood shifted. She became like a venomous serpent. "Then go, you son of a bitch!" She got up and quickly hurried away from him, toward the front of the main lounge.

Martin Wallace let her go. This scene, or its variation, had been played between them many times before.

With a sigh, Martin started toward the corridor that led to the rear of the plane. Frank Powers stood there waiting for him. He had seen what had transpired between Martin Wallace and his wife. It was not the first time he had witnessed such an incident. The two men looked at each other, and a bond of silent understanding passed between them. Frank knew how much Martin Wallace loved Karen, and he knew the pain that Wallace was feeling. Together the two men headed to the communications room to help Dr. Williams.

Lisa leaned against an overturned sofa. She cradled Benjy in her arms. The little boy couldn't help seeing the Wallaces argue. Then, he had seen Mr. Wallace leave with Frank Powers. There was something about what he had seen that had scared him. He looked up at his mother, who stroked his hair and smiled down at him.

"Mama..."

"What, dear?"

"Are we all going to die?"

Lisa hugged Benjy to her. She could sense the little boy's confusion about what was happening. Death was still a barely comprehensible phenomenon to him, yet he knew that it represented something awful.

"No, dear," Lisa said. "We're all going to be all right. You just wait and see." She hugged Benjy even closer to her, and tried to stop the tears from welling up in her eyes.

126

Gallagher and Buchek took two flashlights from the emergency locker and headed down the stairs that led from the main lounge to the lower level of the plane. It was pitch-black in the lower deck, and when Gallagher turned his flashlight on, he saw that the area at the foot of the stairs was flooded. They continued on down, and stepped off the stairs into the knee-deep water. Buchek shone his flashlight around him. There were a number of huge bulges in the aluminum skin of the plane, as well as a number of riveted joints that looked as though they might pop at any time. Gallagher moved the beam of his flashlight around him. In the beam he caught the body of the chef, floating facedown in the water. He moved the beam of his flashlight along the wall until he found the circuit-breaker box. He sloshed through the water, opened the breaker box, and reset the switches that were inside. Dimly, the emergency lights came on throughout the lower level. Checking the fuselage as they went, Gallagher and Buchek headed through the crew seating area, which appeared to be damaged in the same way other parts of the plane were. Seats were uprooted, and debris was everywhere. They moved on, to the bulkhead that separated the crew seating area from the forward cargo hold.

Buchek knelt down and felt the bottom of the cargo-hold door. The rubber seal at the bottom of the door was distorted, and a steady stream of seawater was flowing through the seal. Buchek realized they were in very serious trouble.

Gallagher ran his hand up the bulkhead, from floor to ceiling. He turned to Buchek. "Feel that. It's cold all the way up the bulkhead."

Buchek did as Gallagher asked. He shook his head. It meant that the number-one cargo hold was completely flooded. Buchek carefully examined the seal around the bulkhead door. "If any more of that seal goes, we're finished."

Both men understood the seriousness of the situation.

It seemed unlikely that the passenger areas could be kept dry for long. Inevitably the plane would flood. But would rescue come before that happened? It was a question that neither man could answer.

Julie leaned over the ruined bar and searched for a clean bar towel. Finding what she wanted, she hurried back to Steve. He was leaning against the side of the plane, pressing a blood-soaked towel to a deep cut on his face. Julie knelt down and exchanged the towel for a fresh one.

Steve seemed more lucid now and less racked with pain than he had before. Julie was terribly worried for him. She thought how awful the crash must have been for him. It was terrible enough for her and the others, but it must be far worse to be blind and have to experience the pain and tumult without knowing what was happening.

She touched his cheek gently. "How are you feeling?"

Steve smiled, his voice still weak. "I'm a little woozy. I'll be all right, don't worry."

But she was worried, terribly worried. Although she had known Steve only a short while, something about him had touched her. She cared for him so much. And, she had to admit, she knew that something very good could happen between them.

Steve reached out for her, and she took his hand. "I guess I got off lucky, Julie. After the crash, I could hear the people screaming. It sounded bad, real bad." He swallowed, then licked his lips, as if they were parched.

"Can I get you some water?"

"Yeah. Thanks. I can use that."

As Julie started to get up, Steve stopped her with his hand. Then he touched her face, lightly tracing her features. Drawing his hand back, he smiled. "You know, you must be very, very beautiful."

Visibly moved, Julie took his hand in hers and pressed it to her cheek. She hurried to the ruined bar, found an unbroken glass, and filled it from the small amount that still flowed from the tap.

When she returned to Steve, she thought he was sleeping. His face looked relaxed, peaceful, and happy. But as she knelt down next to him, something almost prescient told her the truth. He was dead. She quickly put her head to his chest and confirmed the awful truth. Taking Steve's head against her breast, she began to rock him like a baby, sobbing all the while.

13

Eddie, the bartender, was lying with his back propped against the bulkhead of the communications room. He drained the last of a tall glass of whiskey, held the tumbler out again, and it was refilled from a liquor bottle that Martin Wallace was holding. The pain his leg caused was agonizing, but he noticed that the whiskey he had already drunk was having some effect on it. Concerned, Dr. Williams moved closer to him.

"Drink it down, Eddie."

Eddie nodded obediently, then drank down the entire glassful. He reacted as a wave of nausea hit him, then passed.

"God," Eddie said, "that's awful. I've been a bartender for fifteen years, and I still can't get used to the stuff."

He took another long drink. He was beginning to feel quite drunk and dizzy. He had held his emotions under control for some time now, but the fears he felt for his wife and the child that was coming were surfacing again. His poor wife. He wondered if he would ever see her again. Thinking back to the radio-telephone conversation he had had, he ran his father's words through his mind again, then spoke abruptly.

"Doctor, have you ever heard of plasmic toxemia?" he asked.

Dr. Williams thought for a second. "I'm not sure, but I think its a condition in pregnancy that's very dangerous for both the mother and the child. Why do you ask?"

Eddie just shook his head. There was no reason to impose his problems on these people. They had problems enough of their own.

"No reason," he said. "I just wanted to know." He took another drink of whiskey. The room swirled before his eyes, and he knew that he was incredibly drunk. He was dimly aware of the fact that the doctor had begun working on his broken leg. The pain became agony, then grew to such an extent that it was a tender mercy when he lost consciousness.

Gallagher and Buchek sloshed through the water in the lower level of the plane. They had finished their inspection.

Gallagher turned to Buchek. "Okay, we know where all the major weak spots are. What's your evaluation?"

Buchek had given this considerable thought. "The middle and rear cargo holds are dry. There's some distortion of the fuselage down here, but I think the major problem is the leak in the forward-cargo-hold door."

"Any way we can plug it up?"

"No. Too much pressure."

"How long till the lower level of the plane is completely flooded?" Gallagher asked.

Buchek made a quick mental calculation. "I don't think the lower level will fill in less than two to three hours. Rescue *has* to get here before then."

"That calculation's fine," Gallagher said. "*If* rescue gets here by then, and *if* we don't spring any more leaks."

Buchek was about to reply, when Crawford appeared at the head of the stairs. "Captain," he said, "the copilot's regained consciousness."

Gallagher felt a little relief at this news. The things he would learn from Chambers could be of critical importance to their survival. Followed by Buchek, he moved through the water and mounted the stairs to the main lounge.

Benjy sat cuddled in his mother's arms. He watched as Gallagher and Buchek hurried across the main lounge to the flight-deck stairs. He turned to his mother. "Is the pilot going to rescue us now?"

"They're working on it, darling."

Benjy nodded. "That means we'll get to see Grandpa soon, doesn't it?"

"Yes, dear."

"What's Grandpa like?" Benjy asked. There was real curiosity in the little boy's voice.

Lisa laughed and stroked her son's curly brown hair. "Oh, he's tall," she said wistfully. "And sometimes he smokes a pipe that smells very nice. And when he laughs, it makes you feel like laughing."

Benjy hesitated for a moment. "Does he yell a lot when he gets mad? Like Mrs. Wallace?"

Lisa was puzzled. "Benjy, what makes you think he gets mad a lot?"

"The way you talked about him, I thought he did."

Lisa smiled, then gave Benjy a hug. "Oh, Benjy, he only gets mad a little bit. And even then, I don't think he really means it."

Chambers was severely bruised and battered, but he was not seriously hurt. He sat up on the couch in the office and answered Gallagher's questions as Eve, Buchek, and Crawford listened.

Chambers' explanations sickened Gallagher. The hijacking, the gas, the guns, the whole thing was so sordid, so unnecessary. As the story unfolded, Gallagher again felt his anger growing. But he still had important questions to ask, and he managed to keep his feelings under control.

"Did coastal radar have a fix on us before the crash?"

Chambers shook his head. "No. There wasn't a chance of that. We were flying too low for radar interception."

Furious, Gallagher hauled Chambers up by his lapels and spoke directly into his face. "It's very fortunate you're injured, you miserable son of a bitch, or I'd take you apart." He let go of Chambers' lapels, and the man sank back onto the couch. Gallagher turned to Crawford. "Get him downstairs, where we can keep an eye on him."

Still angry, Gallagher left the office and moved to the

stairs that led to the main lounge. Eve followed him, her face tense with anxiety. She stopped him at the head of the stairs. "What does it mean, Don?"

He looked around to make sure they wouldn't be overheard, then spoke quietly. "It means that Chambers took us a couple of hundred miles off our flight plan. The search planes won't even be looking for us here."

Eve could barely believe what she was hearing. "There's no chance they'll find us, then?"

Gallagher shook his head. "Not a chance in hell. We're on our own."

The intensity with which the Navy Tactical Coordination Center pursued the missing 747 had not decreased. But as the night grew on, and only negative reports from the search jets filtered in, the men at the center began to show the strain and depression that accompanied an apparently fruitless search.

Coffee was being consumed by the gallon, and ashtrays were filled with cigarette butts. Admiral Corrigan, his jacket off and his necktie loosened, divided his time between the weather printout machine and the chart table. The weather was worsening rapidly, and he was trying to coordinate the ongoing search pattern with the incoming weather, rerouting search jets into the areas that were immediately threatened by mist and fog. He knew that if they did not search those areas before they were enveloped by the fog, then they wouldn't be able to locate a battleship there, much less a downed aircraft.

But as, one by one, the squares were marked off the chart in grease pencil, the atmosphere in the room became tenser. Corrigan had hoped that he would have news of a sighting, or at least some hope to offer Philip Stevens when he arrived in Jacksonville from Palm Beach. But by the time the man had arrived and had been driven to the center, Corrigan had no more to tell him than he had during their phone conversation a little over an hour before.

Philip Stevens took this lack of progress stoically. He

sat down in a folding chair in the planning room, and Corrigan outlined to him what had been done so far. Stevens just nodded.

Stevens was still getting over the shock of the plane's disappearance. He had always felt himself equipped to deal with any kind of catastrophe. Emotionally, he was very tough. But it was this agonizing waiting, the slow prolongation of any concrete word as to what had happened. It was the terrible uncertainty that he felt eating at him. He knew that Corrigan, who was his friend, would do everything in his power to find the plane. And he could tell from the efficient bustle and noise in the planning room that these men were not just doing their job, they were dedicated to their work. He knew, essentially, that Corrigan and his men would do everything humanly possible to save his friends.

But he also knew that that might not be enough. It was as though whatever might happen to his friends lay with luck as much as with the effort expended by the rescuers. Call it fate, or call it destiny, he could only hope that somehow he would see the passengers on that plane again. But most dear to him, of course, were Lisa and Benjy.

The thought that his daughter and grandson might be dead tore into him with almost physical force. Losing them would be almost too much for him to bear. Even a man as tough as Philip Stevens had his limits, and he had reached them.

Stevens shook his head, trying to clear a sudden wave of exhaustion that came over him.

Corrigan saw that his friend was feeling bad and moved to him. "Come on," he said. "Let's get some fresh air." He helped Stevens up, and the two of them walked through the crowded and smoke-filled room to an exit door.

When they were outside, Philip Stevens breathed deep and immediately began to feel better. Although there was some overcast, he could see stars in the clear portion of the sky. Adjoining the Tactical Coordination Center was the naval airfield.

Under the bright airfield lights, Stevens could see two swift S-3 search jets being refueled. He heard a sudden roar and saw another search jet streak across the field and take off into the night sky. Seeing the plane head off to the search, Stevens felt reassured. He turned to Admiral Corrigan.

"Herb, I want you to level with me. What are our chances?"

Corrigan looked at Philip Stevens and knew he had to tell him the truth. "Between the Navy and the Coast Guard, we've got twenty planes in the air and six ships at sea. So far, they've come up with absolutely nothing." Corrigan took out a cigarette and lit it. He took a deep drag on the cigarette and exhaled smoke explosively. "Absolutely goddamn nothing," he said angrily. "I'm sorry, Phil. It doesn't look good. It doesn't look good at all."

Although Philip Stevens had been trying to prepare himself for words such as these, hearing them was another matter. Corrigan's words made his heart sink. He almost crumpled under their impact. Then he gritted his teeth and forced himself to stand up as straight as he could. "My daughter and grandson are on that plane," he said softly. "Did you know that?"

Corrigan shook his head in the affirmative.

Stevens reached into his coat pocket and took out his wallet. He opened it and extracted a picture of Lisa. He looked at it fondly. "You don't have any children, do you, Herb?"

"No. But I think I appreciate what you're going through right now."

"Thank you," Philip Stevens said. He handed the picture to Corrigan, who looked at it. The picture was of a beautiful young woman standing near a horse. Perched on top of the horse was a little boy wearing a cowboy hat.

"She's a beautiful girl," Corrigan said. He was greatly moved by the emotions that Stevens was sharing with him. Stevens took the picture back and gazed at it again. It seemed to remind him of the many years that Lisa had spent with him, growing up. And, just as bitterly, it reminded him of the years between them that he had been robbed of because of the senseless anger that had grown between them. If only he could see her again. If only by some miracle the plane could be found, and Lisa and Benjy were safe!

Stevens felt a hand on his arm. It was Corrigan. There was a determined look on his face. "We'll keep searching, Phil. We're going to find that plane, I promise you."

Philip Stevens nodded. He looked off into the dark Florida sky, out toward the ocean. They *had* to keep searching. Somewhere out there, he knew, somewhere out there were Lisa and Benjy and the rest of them, waiting searching.

Somewhere...

There was a heavy atmosphere of gloom in the main lounge of the submerged 747. The passengers were exhausted, and many of them slept. Others were clustered together in small groups, talking quietly and seeking relief from their terror in human companionship. There was little to do now. What attention and aid could be given the injured had been done, and much of the shattered glass and debris that had littered the lounge had been pushed safely out of the way.

An eerie greenish light seeped through the windows of the lounge. It was now nearing dawn, and the first rays of the new day's sun penetrated down through the water. At first, this had raised the spirits of the passengers. They had clustered around the windows to see the signs of light outside. They hadn't realized that so much time had passed. It would soon be daytime, and they all thought that the plane would have a greater chance of being spotted. And there was, they recognized, the animal instinct that welcomed the daylight and left them feeling a little less abandoned and lost than they had felt when surrounded by the blackness of night.

Much had happened in the hours before dawn. For one thing, Gallagher had explained to them a good deal of what had occurred—the gassing, the guns brought on board, the hijacking, with the theft of art goods as the motive. The passengers' first response was simply stunned silence. Then there was a growing and ugly anger, directed at Chambers, who sat, stooped and suddenly insignificant, by himself in the main lounge. Lucas moved to strike Chambers, but Gallagher grabbed him and held him back. "We're not going to turn into some kind of mob," Gallagher told them. "The authorities will deal with Chambers when the rescue units get here. Now that it's light, they'll spot us in no time."

Gallagher didn't like lying to the passengers, but he felt he had little choice. He had made a number of excuses for the delay in rescue. The most believable one was that weather conditions and darkness had prevented the fullest possible search. The tension in the main lounge had grown, and he calculated that if the guests knew that there wasn't a prayer of the plane being found, the result would be a full-scale panic. Gallagher didn't want to tell them the truth about their situation until he could, at the same time, offer them some hope. He had an ace up his sleeve. But he'd have to go over the plane's electrical schematics with Buchek first. If what he was looking for proved to be correct, it would mean that there was a way they could help themselves. It would be an extremely dangerous way—but a way, nonetheless. So he tried to reassure them that help was on its way. But even as he spoke, he sensed the continuing uneasiness of the passengers. He recognized that, in an emotional sense at least, they knew something was wrong with his explanations. Soon they would be asking questions that he couldn't answer. Before that, he had to have evidence that his plan would work.

After Gallagher had sufficiently calmed the passengers, he hurried to Buchek and told him of his plan. The two of them went to the cockpit and returned with the plane's wiring-schematics book.

And now, in the rear of the main lounge, Buchek and Gallagher had been poring over the large volume for the past forty-five minutes. There was little noise in the plane.

As time passed, the guests became even quieter, partly from sheer physical exhaustion and partly from the tremendous emotional strain they were all under. All that was heard for a long while was an occasional moan or the murmur of someone in a troubled sleep.

Eventually, exhaustion won out over intense pain, and Dorothy had been able to slip into an uneasy sleep. Emily cradled her head in her lap and gently stroked Dorothy's cheek. Dorothy's suffering had torn at Emily's heart. The two women had been friends and companions for so long that her compassion for Dorothy was the same she would have felt for any close member of her family. In fact, Dorothy was as much a part of her family as any of her blood relations. They had been together for so long that the two women could almost communicate without using any words.

A sigh issued from Dorothy's lips, and her eyes fluttered open. As she awoke, Emily daubed at her fevered forehead with a wet compress.

"Does that feel better?" Emily asked.

Dorothy nodded. It was difficult for her to talk, and as she spoke, the words came out weakly. Emily had to lean forward to hear what she was saying.

"Is Mr. St. Downs the man you used to talk about?" she asked.

Emily was surprised. "Why, that was years and years ago. How on earth did you remember that?"

Dorothy smiled. "You used to keep his picture in the study."

"That's right."

"He's very handsome," Dorothy said. She gave Emily a meaningful look. "Is he married?"

Emily was amused. Dorothy had always insisted that Emily was happier married than not. She was constantly on the lookout for prospective suitors. Even now she was an incurable matchmaker.

Emily just smiled. "That's enough talk for now," she said to Dorothy. "What you need is rest."

Dorothy closed her eyes and soon she was asleep again.

Someone knelt next to Emily. It was Dr. Williams. "How is she?" he asked Emily.

"In pain. Isn't there anything that you can give her?"

Williams shook his head. "I'm afraid not. I wish I had some sedatives, but I don't." Emily could hear the frustration in his voice.

Williams put a hand on her shoulder and got up. He made his way across the lounge, stopping to check on the little girl, who was resting comfortably. Then he moved to the other side of the lounge. Eddie had been brought in and placed on a sofa. Nicholas St. Downs sat beside him. Eddie's leg was bandaged and held immobile with splints that they had made by breaking out the slats of a chair.

A smile appeared on Eddie's face when he saw Dr. Williams. He was still quite woozy from all the liquor he had consumed. But he wanted to talk to Dr. Williams, to thank him. He extended his hand, and Williams shook it, then sat down next to Eddie.

"How are you feeling?"

"A lot better, a whole hell of a lot better."

Williams looked down at Eddie's leg. There was no further bleeding, and the splint was secure. Williams felt proud of the work he had done. It had been an awful fracture, but if somehow they were rescued, Eddie would have full use of that leg again.

"Doctor, I want to thank you."

"No thanks are necessary, Eddie."

"But I want to thank you anyway. You must be the best doctor in Palm Beach."

"Well," said Williams, "maybe not the best doctor, but certainly the best veterinarian." There was a noticeable pause, and Eddie's jaw dropped a little. "Doc, you're putting me on."

"Not at all," said Williams. "I take care of Mr. Stevens' racehorses at Hialeah."

"Jesus Christ," was all Eddie could say. He grinned. "Jesus Christ," he said again, and started laughing.

"Let's keep that as our little secret, right?" Dr. Williams said.

"Right," said Eddie. He was still laughing to himself as Dr. Williams got up and went off to check the other injured passengers.

"Where's the E-15 circuit?" Gallagher asked. Buchek leaned forward to get a better look at the page. He and Gallagher were still seated in a corner of the main lounge, going over the incredibly complicated electrical-wiring diagrams for the rear cargo areas of the 747. Buchek looked through the color-coded diagrams, found the E-15 circuit, and traced it with his forefinger.

"Right there."

"Got it," Gallagher said, nodding. "Is it accessible? Can we tap into it?"

"Sure. Just rip away the panel and split the conduit."

Gallagher grinned. "Hank, you almost make it sound easy."

"Natural genius," Buchek said. He pointed to another circuit diagram on the page. "Now, if you want to tap in here . . ."

A drop of water splattered on the page. Then, three more. Buchek looked up.

There, on the ceiling, water was beginning to collect. It was only a film at the moment, but for the first time, water was beginning to penetrate the main lounge.

Buchek and Gallagher exchanged looks. "I'll be right back," Buchek said. As Gallagher went back to work on the electrical diagrams, Buchek got up and walked calmly to the stairs that led to the flight deck of the aircraft. As he neared the top of the stairs, he heard it. It was faint, barely discernible, but it was quite clearly the sound of water. Water was beginning to find its way into the passenger areas of the aircraft.

Buchek went to the office door. The carpeting beneath his feet was soaked. Grimly he opened the door to the office.

It was bad. A steady stream of water poured down the wall. It was obvious that one of the plane's seams was beginning to leak. He watched as the water crept along the floor, darkening the carpet as it flowed into the room.

Mother of God, Buchek thought to himself. How long did they have now? How much longer before the plane started to crack under the pressure of the ocean?

Buchek closed the door to the office. He went into the cockpit and picked up an oxygen mask and cylinder, then started back down the stairs. Gallagher's plan was crazy. But it looked like it was their only chance.

Buchek came down the stairs and into the main lounge. He walked swiftly over to Gallagher and put the oxygen cylinder and mask on an unoccupied seat. As Buchek sat down next to him, Gallagher looked up from the schematics book.

"It's started," Buchek said.

"How bad?"

"Plenty. How're you doing?"

Gallagher pointed to an area on the page. "I want to take a look at the 57W circuit."

Buchek nodded. Whatever they did, they'd have to do it soon. Somehow he could not shake out of his mind what he had seen. He thought of the seawater that was slowly and surely making its way into the plane. It was a small stream, but steady, and he knew just as surely as his name was Hank Buchek that if they didn't find a way out of the 747, that water would eventually drown them all.

14

For a long time after Steve's death, Julie had been able to bear up very well. There had been so much work to be done, so many people to help, that she had gratefully thrown herself into whatever duties she could find, and had deliberately avoided examining her feelings. In fact, it had been almost like putting her feelings in some secret compartment of her being, a compartment where grief could be completely outside of her awareness. But now, with most of the injured taken care of, and nothing to do but sit and wait, Julie's defenses against her feelings had fallen.

She had been immensely grateful that Eve Clayton had seen her, sitting alone, with only her grief to keep her company. Eve had come over and begun to talk to her. Little by little, the two women talked about it, until Julie's feelings of grief and loss came completely to the surface. Then Eve had just held her and soothed her until she had gotten most of the crying out of her system. Wiping away her tears with a handkerchief that Eve had given her, Julie began to speak again. This time, she was more composed and more on her way to a clearer understanding of her feelings.

"I didn't know him well, Eve. But somehow I felt he really understood me. More than anyone ever has before."

"Well," Eve said, "that's one advantage blind people have. They see a lot more than the surface."

Julie nodded, thinking about what Eve had said. Tears began to mist her eyes again. "Do you know what I wish?"

"What?"

"That I'd met him a long, long time ago."

Eve looked at her with knowing compassion.

Suddenly, a puzzled expression, one that was half curious, half full of fear, came over Julie's face.

Concerned, Eve grasped Julie's shoulders. "Julie, what's wrong?"

"Listen," Julie said. "Don't you hear that noise? What is it?"

Eve listened carefully. Soon she heard it too. It was something between a noise and a vibration. Eve strained her ears. She got up and called excitedly to the others in the main lounge. "Everyone. Please. Be quiet for a second. Listen!"

The guests gave Eve puzzled looks, then, one by one, fell silent. Soon it was totally quiet in the main lounge, and it was possible to hear the noise. The noise continued. It seemed to be coming from outside, and it was growing louder.

Martin Wallace got to his feet and listened carefully. His mind was racing, and he was becoming terribly excited. He had scuba-dived extensively, and the sound he heard was one that was totally familiar to him. Smiling now, he spoke out loud to the entire group. "It's a ship. That's the sound of a ship! They're coming for us!"

There were cries of thankfulness and relief at this news. Some of the guests hugged each other, others moved to the windows and tried to see outside. But all that was visible was the same murky green water they'd seen since the sun had risen.

On the surface of the water, the French oil tanker *Liberté* plowed through the ocean at a steady fifteen knots. The oil tanker rode high in the water, because it was carrying only a small amount of water as ballast. The ship was on its way around the tip of Florida to take on a load of crude oil at Galveston, Texas. The tanker pitched and bobbed in the rough seas, and the crew looked forward to their arrival at their destination. They had

144

been at sea for a long time, and were bored and ready to set foot on land again. Also, they knew that once they took on a load of crude oil, the ship would ride much better and they would have a less unpleasant journey on their return trip.

On the ship's bridge, the morning watch went on placidly. The master of the watch noted that the broken storm clouds allowed glimpses of the rising sun and promised a beautiful sunrise. He sipped coffee, lit his first cigarette of the day, and relaxed in his seat. The word had gone out on the rescue channels that a 747 had been lost. But as the big ship plowed along, he saw nothing but the endless rolling ocean. There was, of course, nothing to see on the surface of the water.

The throbbing sound of the ship's engines diminished inside the main lounge of the 747. A murmur of fear and hopelessness ran through the group of guests, who, only a short time ago, had felt such joy. The guests became totally silent, hoping beyond hope that the ship was not really going away. But soon the sound of its engines faded away into nothingness.

Lisa held Benjy tightly. The intense strain that she felt showed in her face. She turned to Buchek and voiced the question that all the other guests had in their minds as well. "How could they just leave us here? How could they?"

Buchek stood in the center of the lounge, clenching his fist. His whole body was filled with tension. He shook his head and answered Lisa grimly. "I don't know. I can't explain it."

Angrily, Karen Wallace moved closer to the center of the main lounge. She looked at the rest of the guests with contempt, then turned to Buchek. "I know why they didn't stop. Do you really want to know?"

Everyone in the lounge fell silent and listened to Karen with interest. As she spoke, her words were dripping with hatred and accusation. "They didn't stop because they never saw us. It was just a passing ship. They didn't even know we were here. Haven't you idiots figured it out yet? *They'll never find us!" Nobody* knows we're here!"

Karen's words were followed by a shocked silence. She presented a reality that seemed inevitable, yet it had been a reality that every one of the guests had been trying to put out of his mind. The guests could no longer ignore the obvious truth that Karen's words suggested.

Suddenly the silence was broken by Lisa. Clutching her little boy to her, she began to cry, her voice breaking into deep racking sobs.

Gallagher had watched Karen with distaste. The last thing in the world he wanted was a panic, but obviously Karen Wallace was the kind of person who alleviated her own anxiety by spreading it around to other people. He moved quickly to her. "I think that's enough, Mrs. Wallace."

"Is it? Why hasn't rescue come, Captain? Just tell me that."

Gallagher realized that he could protect them from the truth no longer. He decided that he would have to level with them, both about the situation they were in and about the possible solution he hoped to attempt.

"All right," he said. "The situation *is* much worse than I told you before. We're far off course. The search planes that are looking for us aren't anywhere near this area. But Mr. Buchek and I have a plan that we think can bring the search planes to us."

He looked around the main lounge and saw the intensity with which the guests were listening to him. Their fear and desperation were at such a height that they were literally grasping at any thread he might offer.

Gallagher went to the cabinet where the life jackets and emergency equipment were kept. He reached in and removed a large bright yellow package. Then, carrying it, he returned to the center of the main lounge and placed the package on the floor at his feet.

"This is a self-inflating life raft. It contains a small radio unit that triggers when the raft is on the surface of the water. It will broadcast a Mayday signal to the rescue units that are looking for us."

Karen Wallace snorted in derision. "On the *surface* of the water? A lot of good that does us down here, Captain."

"That's right," he said. "That's why we're going to try to get this raft out of the plane."

There was a moment of shocked silence as the guests tried to understand how he could possibly hope to get something outside without flooding the plane.

"There's one door on this plane that opens inward. It's in the rear cargo hold. Mr. Buchek and I have been studying the plane's wiring schematics, and we think we can open it electrically. There are two sealed doors between the rear cargo hold and here. *If* the bulkheads and the doors hold, only the rear cargo area will be flooded. I'll be in the rear cargo hold."

"But how will you breathe?" Nicholas St. Downs asked.

In answer to St. Downs, Buchek crossed to the table where he and Gallagher had been working. He reached onto the seat and picked up an oxygen mask and emergency oxygen cylinder that were lying there, then moved forward in the lounge to show them to the guests. St. Downs nodded with dawning understanding.

Gallagher continued, "I'll be in the cargo hold with this oxygen gear. If I can get the raft out and inflate it, Search and Rescue will pick up its radio signal."

Gallagher had finished his speech. Now he just waited for the guests to absorb what he had said and to react.

As Eve listened to Gallagher, his words terrified her. The thought of his being inside the cargo compartment, then deliberately flooding it, was like a claustrophobic nightmare to her. Yet, what choice did he have? If he didn't make an attempt to bring help, they would all surely die.

There was a long silence. Then Nicholas St. Downs spoke, and it was as if he were speaking for the rest of the passengers. "Captain," he said, "I'm sure we all want to know what we can do to help you. Please tell us, and you'll have our full cooperation."

"Thank you," Gallagher said. "I know I will. But right now, Mr. Buchek and I have to go down to the rear cargo area and check the wiring circuits. While we're gone, I'd like to ask you all to just stay calm."

Frightened, Eve reached out and took Gallagher's hand.

He clasped her hand in his for a moment, then turned to Buchek. "Come on, we've got a lot of work to do."

At that moment, Martin Wallace stepped forward. He had been doing a lot of thinking about what Gallagher had said. Now he felt he had to speak. "Captain, I think I should go with you."

Gallagher shook his head. "No. Absolutely not."

Wallace moved closer. "Captain, I'm an experienced scuba diver. What you're going to do will be incredibly dangerous. It's simple mathematics. Two men have a better chance than one."

Gallagher was about to reject Wallace's offer again when Buchek spoke up. "He's right, Don."

Gallagher gave it some thought. Actually, if Wallace wanted to take the risk, what right had he to say no to the man? "All right, Mr. Wallace. Get another mask and oxygen cylinder from the cockpit. We'll be below.

Without another word, Gallagher motioned to Buchek, and carrying the life-raft package and the oxygen equipment, the two men headed down the stairs that led to the lower level of the plane.

Gallagher's words had had an incredible impact on the guests. They knew that there were terrific dangers inherent in the solution that Gallagher had proposed. Yet, the hours of fear and waiting had taken an awful emotional toll on all of them. Now they were anxious for a solution, regardless of the great risks that solution might impose on them.

Nicholas St. Downs came over to Emily Livingston, carrying a paper cup of water. Emily took the cup and sipped from it. "Thank you, Nicky," she said.

St. Downs looked at Dorothy, whose head was cradled in Emily's lap. Dorothy's eyes were closed, and her breathing was uneven. "How is she?" he asked.

"Sleeping. She'll be all right, I hope." Emily took another sip of the water.

St. Downs saw a tear run down her face. He took out his handkerchief and dabbed it away. "Don't cry, my dear. Somehow, I feel we'll make it through this."

Emily turned to him and took his hand. "I'm not crying for us, Nicky," she said. "We've lived long, full lives. I'm crying for the others. Some of them are so young. There are so many joys and disappointments and triumphs that they haven't tasted yet."

St. Downs listened and nodded agreement as she spoke. Then he put his arm around her shoulder and held her to him. "You're right, Emily. Death never cheats the old, only the young."

After they reached the rear cargo compartment, Gallagher and Buchek had immediately stripped a large section of aluminum from the wall and exposed the conduit that carried the electrical wires they were after. Gallagher had unscrewed one of the conduit's joints and exposed the thick sheaf of multi-colored electrical wires. Buchek stood behind Gallagher and cursed silently as Gallagher sorted through the wires, looking for the ones that they wanted. Buchek knew he could do the work much faster himself, but because of his injured arm, he had to content himself with giving directions and letting Gallagher do the actual work. After a few minutes, Eve had come down into the rear cargo hold and joined them. Buchek had pressed her into service, and Eve passed tools to Gallagher and wrapped connections as he worked. Buchek watched carefully as Gallagher reached for two wires. One mistake, and the cargo door might open prematurely.

"That's it," Buchek said. "Twist the red and the green wires together. But don't let them touch the blue one."

Gallagher finished, breathed a sigh of relief, then

backed away from the wires. "How much more?"

Buchek closed the schematics book and placed it on the floor. "That's all there is to it. Just touch those two wires together, and the cargo door will unlock. Outside water pressure should pop it right open."

Gallagher nodded, then motioned toward the wall that separated the cargo hold from the middle portion of the plane. "What worries me is whether that bulkhead will hold. I don't know how much water pressure it can stand up to."

"Well, partner," Buchek said, "that's what we're going to find out, because we sure as hell don't have any other choice."

Martin Wallace clipped the small oxygen cylinder to his belt. Attached to the cylinder was a thin plastic hose that ran to a face mask. Wallace pulled the elastic band of the face mask over his head, then put the mask to his face. He turned the oxygen cylinder on and breathed in. His lungs were flooded with oxygen. He turned the cylinder off. It was extremely primitive equipment. It was designed to provide supplementary oxygen for the flight crew, and certainly was never intended for use underwater. But it would do, considering the circumstances.

He was in the main lounge, stripped to the waist. As he was preparing for the mission, the guests had come up to offer him reassurance and thanks for what he was doing. Lucas, the art critic, had shaken his hand. Mrs. Stern had embraced him, telling him that he was a brave man. Julie Denton, her eyes red from crying, had kissed him warmly on the cheek. It had made Martin Wallace feel good in a way that he had rarely felt in many years. It was a strange, almost mystical communion that he felt with these people.

There was one person who did not speak to him as he prepared his equipment and got ready to go. That was his wife, Karen. After he had volunteered to go with Gallagher, he and Karen had had a brief but bitter quarrel. He had suspected that he would have to leave without saying good-bye to her. So now, as he headed for the stairs that led to the lower level of the plane, he was surprised when he saw her move toward him. He felt a surge of emotion. Whatever she had become, she was still his wife. There had been a time, he knew, when their relationship hadn't been the poisonous tangle it now was.

Karen put her arms out and embraced him. She then pulled away and looked him straight in the eyes. "Nothing I can say will make a difference, will it?"

Martin Wallace didn't respond. All that could have been said between them had been said. He felt the tension in her hands and felt her nails dig into his arm.

"Let Gallagher go! Don't risk your life!" she said.

Somehow, before he went, he wanted to make Karen see how wrong she was. If only, for once, she might see that her selfishness was self-destructive and was maiming her and everyone around her.

"Karen," he said, "can't you see I'm doing this for all of us?"

"Us!" Karen snarled contemptuously. "We're us. You and I. That's all. All those other people are a bunch of strangers. Oh, Martin, that's always been your problem. You think everybody is us. For once, forget about the others. Forget about everyone. For God's sake, think of yourself!"

"People who thought only of themselves got us down here, Karen," Martin said.

He shook himself loose from her hands. There was no way of making her understand. There was no point, really, in even trying.

Karen looked at her husband with great sadness. She shook her head. "You've got a lot of brains, Martin. But you're not a smart man." Then, suddenly angry, she said, "Go on, then! Be a goddamn martyr. But don't expect me to applaud your cheap heroics!"

Her eyes flooded with tears as she ran from him toward the rear of the main lounge. Martin Wallace watched her go with genuine sadness and pain in his heart. But he knew there was nothing more he could say. He had to go.

He didn't regret his decision, but suddenly he felt very alone. He turned and went down the stairs that led to the lower level and the cargo holds.

Frank Powers was in the kitchen area, up to his knees in water. He had been helping Gallagher and Buchek remove the lighter and smaller boxes from the cargo hold, and had helped them tie down the cargo that was too large to be removed. As he saw Martin come down the stairs, wearing the makeshift scuba gear, he knew that the time for farewells had arrived. The two old friends shook hands. Frank was very moved. Martin Wallace, in many ways, had been like a father to him. The guilt of what he had done with Karen Wallace hung over him like a disease, and it seemed wrong that, on what might be their last meeting together, there should be this deceit on Frank's part toward Martin.

Martin clasped Frank to him. "If anything happens to me, I want you to carry on the work. Do you understand?"

"Of course," said Frank.

"And, Frank, if you could, try to make sure Karen doesn't harm herself. Watch over her, please." Despite all she had put him through, Martin Wallace still loved her. Or at least the memory of what she had been.

"Martin?"

"What?"

"About Karen and me..."

"I know about you two," Martin Wallace said. "She came to me and told me almost immediately. She wanted to hurt me with that information. She succeeded. But I've come to believe it was only a moment of weakness on both your parts."

"So you've known all along," Frank said.

"You wonder why I said or did nothing?" Wallace asked. "There's a very simple explanation, really. We're all weak in one way or another. Every human being is. I don't like what happened between you and Karen, but I have to weigh it against all the years we've been friends. In the balance, I still think you've been the best friend a man could have. Forget about what happened between you and Karen. I have."

"Thank you, Martin." Powers was moved almost to tears. He shook hands with Wallace again; then Wallace turned and made his way toward the rear cargo hold.

As Wallace entered the cargo hold, he saw Eve, Gallagher, and Buchek standing near the wall of the hold discussing some last-minute instructions about what to do after Gallagher had gotten out of the aircraft.

As Wallace approached them, he suddenly began to feel a surge of excitement. He was once again going to be challenging the ocean. Rapidly he began to anticipate that old feeling of freedom that being in the sea had always given him. He would be able to forget Karen, his problems, everything. He would be one with the sea again.

Gallagher turned and saw Wallace approach. He gave Wallace the A-OK sign. Wallace returned the gesture and smiled at him.

Gallagher turned to Eve. They had not said much to each other since Gallagher had divulged his plan to the passengers. Their excuse had been that there was no time. This was partly true. But the real reason was that both Gallagher and Eve knew that an emotional scene between them would be too painful. They had to maintain their emotional reserves for the remainder of the ordeal that both knew lay ahead. Still, there had been a deep and unspoken feeling between them, and now, with Martin Wallace here, and the dangerous plan ready to be put into operation, they both felt an extraordinary warmth for each other. Holding back her tears, Eve said, "We've got a date tonight in Palm Beach, right?"

"That's a promise," Gallagher said. He managed a smile, and then took Eve in his arms. They let down their emotional guards long enough to share a deep, long kiss, and she realized how truly happy she felt when she was with him. Then they broke apart, and she looked into his blue eyes. His eyes were now filled with emotion, and he pulled her to him for another embrace. Then, before she began crying, Eve turned and left the cargo hold.

Gallagher turned to Buchek. His old friend reached out his hand, and the two of them shook.

"I guess there isn't a hell of a lot left to say, is there, Hank?" said Gallagher.

"Sure there is," Buchek said. "There just isn't enough time to say it."

There wasn't. Buchek turned to Martin Wallace and wished him luck. Then, obviously trying to hide the deep emotions he felt, the scrappy little man left the cargo hold. Gallagher followed him to the door, and when Buchek had exited, Gallagher closed the door with a thud. He then threw the lever that locked the door and dogged it firmly in place.

Gallagher turned and walked back to Martin Wallace. For a moment both men stood facing the inward-opening cargo door. They were conscious that on the other side of that door was thousands of tons of seawater that they were going to let come crashing torrentially down on them.

"Okay," said Gallagher. "Let's get ready. Get as far away from this cargo door as you can, and find something to hold on to. When that door opens, you're going to think the gates of hell have broken loose."

Martin Wallace nodded and moved away from the door. He found an exposed structural member to hold on to. Gallagher moved to the side of the plane where the wiring was exposed. He fitted his oxygen mask into place and turned on the valve. There was a hiss, and then the cold, clean taste of oxygen was in his lungs. He turned to Wallace. "Ready?"

Wallace was making sure the oxygen cylinder was firmly clipped to his belt. He nodded. "Captain. As we go to the surface, be sure to let air out of your lungs all the way to the top. Don't try to hold your breath, or you'll risk injuring your lungs. The change in pressure between here and the surface will be tremendous." Gallagher nodded in response. Wallace fit his face mask into place, then turned on his oxygen cylinder.

154

Gallagher saw that Wallace was ready. He reached down and took the two sets of wires in his hands. Then he crossed the wires and held them together. There was a grinding sound as the motors that operated the cargo door came into operation. The overhead lights in the cargo hold dimmed. But the cargo door did not move. Gallagher waited a moment, then crossed the wires again. They heard the sound of the motors, but again the door didn't budge.

"What's wrong?" Martin Wallace asked.

Gallagher shook his head in frustration. "The latches must be stuck. Either that or there isn't enough power left in the batteries to open them. Keep your grip on that beam. I'm going to try it again." He put the wires together and held them tightly. The grinding noise started, but nothing happened. Desperately he tried to form a plan, seek some solution to this problem. He looked up from the wiring and saw that Martin Wallace had crossed to the door to investigate the latches.

"Watch it!" Gallagher shouted. "Don't get too close, or . . ."

But it was too late. Apparently the door had worked its way free. Then, pressed by the tons of water outside, the door suddenly flew open and up. It happened so incredibly fast that Gallagher could barely see what happened. But he had seen enough. Martin Wallace took the impact of the door full force, and with a sickening crunch was slammed by the door clear across the cargo hold. Before Gallagher could move, the cargo compartment had become a savage caldron of raging water.

His only thought was for the yellow-life-raft package that was on the floor beside him. Before he could reach for it, the incredible force of the water had knocked him off his feet. Gallagher went spinning against the side of the hull, and the life-raft package was swept away from him. Gallagher's oxygen mask was torn away from him, and suddenly he was gulping seawater instead of air. Then suddenly the entire compartment was filled. He held his breath, and it felt as if his lungs were going to burst.

Gallagher opened his eyes. There was little light coming in from outside the compartment, and the seawater burned his eyes. He felt around him, became conscious of bubbles rising through the water, and in that way found his oxygen gear. Gallagher pressed the oxygen mask to his face and gratefully took in great gulps of air. Then he swam over to Martin Wallace.

Wallace lay floating near the floor of the cargo hold. Gallagher reached him and grabbed him under the arms. But Wallace's head hung limply, his eyes open and unseeing. Gallagher swam with the body to the open cargo-hold door. When the little light that entered the cargo hold shone on Martin Wallace's face, Gallagher knew instantly that nothing could be done for the man. Reluctantly Gallagher moved away from the body and swam deeper into the cargo hold, searching for the yellow-life-raft package.

After Gallagher and Wallace had locked themselves in the rear cargo hold, the passengers had gathered by the windows of the main lounge, hoping desperately that the two men would successfully get out of the plane and safely into the ocean. They could tell when Gallagher crossed the two wires, because the lights throughout the plane had dimmed, and the sound of the cargo-hatch motors could be heard. Their tension increased each time the lights dimmed and they heard the motor noise, because they knew that something must be wrong, that for some reason the hatch was refusing to open.

Then they could feel the cargo hatch open explosively. The plane rocked with the Promethean force of the water roaring into the hold. They held their breath then, waiting to see if the bulkheads would hold.

Buchek had been on the stairs that led to the lower level of the plane. He watched the bulkheads to see how they would take the pressure of the water as it entered the cargo hold. The bulkheads had bulged and strained, but so far they seemed to be holding. Satisfied that the plane would hold together a little longer, he hurried to join the other passengers at the windows of the main lounge.

The next stage of the drama would be enacted outside the plane. The passengers peered as far as they could through the murky water. Then Eve Clayton cried out as she saw a heavy stream of bubbles rolling up toward the surface. What came into view was the life-raft package. As it rose, it expanded and took on the shape of a life raft. With meteoric speed it rose to the surface of the water, far above them. There was a gasp from the passengers as the life raft passed. Then, with great anxiety they now searched for Gallagher and Martin Wallace.

Next, Gallagher appeared. He had tossed aside his oxygen cylinder, and he rose to the surface slowly, expelling air as he went.

As Eve watched Gallagher swim to the surface, she felt a surge of incredible happiness. Don had made it! She grabbed hold of the person nearest her, who happened to be Ralph Crawford, and hugged him.

Suddenly Karen Wallace screamed.

Martin Wallace's body had floated out of the cargo hold. Drifting with the ocean currents, it floated up the side of the 747 and now passed directly in front of the plane's windows.

The impact the door had made on Martin's face was now apparent, for his face was little more than a livid bruise, his features barely discernible. His eyes popped from what had once been his face, and his body was contorted into an unnatural and grotesque position. It all suggested an incredibly painful and grim death.

Frank Powers rushed to Karen, who was sobbing uncontrollably. But she screamed and struck out at him. Lisa tried to go to her, but Karen shouted at her. "Stay away from me, all of you. Leave me alone!" Karen quickly regained control of herself. She gave the guests a condemning look, as if what had happened to her husband had been their fault, then stalked away from them and sat down by herself at the end of the main lounge.

There was a silence in the main lounge. Gallagher

157

might be on the surface, and if the beeper in the life raft was working, rescue might come. But the sight of the dead Martin Wallace reminded them that they still had no guarantee the rescue could arrive in time, or that it would be successful.

When Gallagher broke the surface of the water, he gasped in huge lungfuls of air. The waves were choppy, and there was a considerable swell to the water. So he found it hard going to get to the raft, which seemed nearby but always remained tantalizingly out of reach. He swam hard toward the raft, and after swallowing what seemed like a gallon of seawater, his chest aching and his eyes burning from his ordeal, he managed to reach the raft and haul himself into it. He was so exhausted and cold that all he could do for that first moment was to lie on his back and stare overhead at the sky above him. There was a stiff wind, and the clouds were flattened out. Gallagher shivered. Then, regaining his strength, he checked the beeper unit. To his relief, a low but steady beep-beep-beep sound issued from it. Thank God, Gallagher thought to himself, thank God. His every joint aching, he hauled himself into a sitting position. He looked around him. But as far as his eyes could see, there was only the infinite ocean. There was only one thing left to do now. To wait. And hope.

15

The radioman's mind had begun to wander. He had been sitting at his radio console at the Tactical Coordination Center for some hours now. He had been assigned the job of scanning the emergency channels. He did his job with ease, almost automatically. But since nothing had come over the channels in the hours he'd been monitoring them, he certainly didn't expect anything to come over them now. That was why he was so incredibly startled when the faint Mayday signal began coming in over his radio set. The continuous beeping sound became stronger as he adjusted his set. The Mayday was coming in on the aircraft frequencies, and he hoped that the signal was coming from the lost 747. Excited, he called out the news. "I've got a beeper!" Then he hit the action button on his console. Soon he was surrounded by sailors and officers who wanted to hear the Mayday signal for themselves.

Stevens stood at the command console with Admiral Corrigan. He was confused by all the sudden activity. When Corrigan explained that it meant possible contact with the 747, Stevens felt his hopes rise for the first time.

Corrigan watched as his men tracked the beeper and quickly triangulated its position. Within a few minutes they had computed the Mayday signal's location, and an ensign was hurrying to the command console with the information. Corrigan and Stevens moved to the chart table and watched as the ensign used navigation rulers to mark off the location of the beeper signal. Corrigan couldn't believe what he was seeing. He turned to Stevens and spoke. "Two hundred miles off course. It's incredible, absolutely incredible." Then Corrigan sprang into action. Now that he had a location to work from, he knew exactly what to do. He motioned to Commander Reed, who joined them at the chart table. Reed whistled when he saw the location of the Mayday signal. "What ships are in that area?" Corrigan asked. "The *Greenwich*, the *Hamilton*, and the *Cayuga*. But they're not part of the operation, sir," Reed said.

"They are now," Corrigan responded. "Get me Admiral James at CINCLANT fleet. Then check with the Coast Guard." Things were being put in motion, and Admiral Corrigan felt a sense of great relief. He didn't yet know what the situation was out there, but finally they had some kind of a chance.

As Stevens looked on, his heart soaring, the efficient machinery of the air-sea rescue command moved into high gear. He listened in as the radiomen notified the search jets of the location of the Mayday signal. The cross talk between the radio operators and the rescue jets was, for him, the sound of hope.

"Search Five. This is Search Base. We have an emergency beeper at coordinates 27 degrees north, 65 degrees west. Proceed and investigate."

There was a squawk of static; then: "This is Search Five. Wilco, out," as the pilot responded. Stevens sat down and listened as, one after another, the search planes were sent off to those coordinates. He suddenly had hope, and that made all the difference in the world.

Buchek was in the lower level of the 747. He had been down there twice since Gallagher had gotten out of the plane. Each time, he had checked the condition of the bulkheads, and it was clear to him that their condition was bad, and quickly worsening. He sloshed through the water as he moved toward the crew seating area. The water had been rising steadily down there, and now it was almost at waist level. He didn't have to go all the way forward in the crew seating area to see why. The seal around the door to the forward cargo hold had ruptured even further. Now water was spurting from the sides and top of the door. Worst of all, there was not a thing he could think to do. Buchek heard footsteps on the stairs that led up to the main lounge. He turned and saw that St. Downs was coming down the stairs. St. Downs halted before stepping into the water and called to Buchek. "Mr. Buchek, isn't there anything I can do to help?"

Sadly Buchek shook his head. "We played our last card when we sent Don out. There isn't a goddamn thing any of us can do now."

The passengers sat in the main lounge waiting. For the first time, they all felt they had some chance of being rescued. It had been twenty minutes since Gallagher had gotten out of the plane and floated to the surface. They wondered how long it would take rescue to come, but now there was at least the certainty that *if* the beeper on the life raft were in working order, rescue would soon be on the way.

The guests sat in small groups, talking quietly. All but Karen Wallace, who sat alone, isolated. Earlier, Frank Powers and others had tried to comfort her, but Karen had refused their words of consolation. As Emily watched her, alone, tight-lipped, she felt great compassion for the woman. She rose and moved toward Karen.

"Mrs. Wallace. Why don't you come sit with us?"

Karen didn't respond. In fact, Emily wasn't really sure that Karen had heard her speak.

"Mrs. Wallace, are you all right?"

A flicker of confusion crossed Karen's face. Her mouth moved, as though forming words, yet she still didn't seem to hear Emily. Emily watched as Karen got up, passed her, and moved toward the center of the lounge. Emily thought that even Karen's movements were strange. She walked as if she were a sleepwalker. Puzzled, Emily watched as Karen moved toward the side of the lounge. Karen seemed to have a destination in mind. But where was she going? Emily watched Karen walk behind Eve

Clayton, who was talking quietly to Lisa. Suddenly Emily understood where Karen Wallace was going and what she was going to do when she got there. Emily shouted to her, horrified. "Stop it! Mrs. Wallace, don't do that!"

Eve Clayton turned around. She was in time to see Karen Wallace moving toward the plane's boarding door. As Karen reached for the door handle, Eve jumped to her feet and ran to stop her. Karen was trying to work the handle release when Eve grabbed her arm and pulled it away from the door.

"You'll kill us all. Get away from that door."

Karen struggled with Eve. Her nails went for Eve's eyes. "Leave me alone. I'm trying to get out."

Eve pulled her away from the door, and Karen began screaming and fighting to get to the door.

"Let go of me. I've got to get out of here!"

Karen, in total hysteria, raked her nails across Eve's face, and Eve realized that there was no way she could continue to control this woman. Eve doubled up her fist and hit Karen in the mouth as hard as she could. Karen fell to the floor, and Eve could feel her fist stinging from the blow she had given.

On the floor, Karen sat up and looked at Eve. She reached her hand to her mouth and felt the blood that was there. Eve's blow had split her lip. Finally Karen began sobbing, her crying sounding as if it came from deep inside her soul. Eve knelt down and put her arm around Karen's shoulder in an attempt to comfort her. Puzzled, Karen spoke. "Why did you do that? Look what you did to me." Eve didn't react. Instead, she continued to try to comfort her, knowing that something was seriously wrong inside Karen Wallace's mind.

The jet pilot of Search Five began slowing down his aircraft. He had reached the coordinates from which the Mayday signal had been received. He banked his plane, pierced the heavy cloud cover, and suddenly saw the ocean below him. The pilot made one or two passes over the area before he spotted the man in the little life raft. It

162

looked like a dot on the vast ocean. He banked his jet, came around again, and made another pass over the life raft, dipping the wings of his plane so the man, who was waving his arms, would know without question that he had been seen. The jet pilot didn't see any debris on the water and decided to go to a higher altitude for a wide-angle view. He again circled the area. This time, he felt his heart begin beating rapidly. He was amazed at what he saw.

Beneath the surface of the water was the obscure outline of a 747. He pressed a stud on his flight console, which dropped a dye marker over the area. Then he flicked on his radio and prepared to give the Tactical Coordination Center news of his siting.

Stevens, Corrigan, and a number of Navy officers and men were gathered around the radio console as the pilot of Search Five made his report, then responded to the questions of the radioman.

"This is Search Five. Have located the aircraft at the coordinates given. One man in a life raft. No other survivors sighted. No debris on the surface of the water. Aircraft is completely submerged."

The radioman made pencil notations as the pilot talked. "Is the fuselage intact?" he asked.

"Roger," the pilot replied. "Appears to be."

"Remain on station until relieved. Search Base, out."

"Search Five. Roger, out."

Corrigan turned to Commander Reed. "I want a stage-one alert on this. Get SH-3 helos ready. Scuba teams, compressors, air-hose packages, medics, medical supplies, the works. Treat this just like a submarine-salvage operation."

Reed saluted and hurried off to put the rescue operation into full swing. Corrigan spoke to the radioman.

"Get me the captain on the USS *Cayuga*. On the double."

"Aye, aye, sir," the radioman said.

As Corrigan waited for the connection with the *Cayuga* to be made, he turned to speak to Stevens. There would be little time for talking, and he knew he'd better answer any of Stevens' questions right now.

"Herb," Stevens said, "is there any chance that there's more than one survivor?"

Corrigan nodded vigorously. "There's a good chance. We've rescued survivors from submerged aircraft before. The hull seems to be intact, and that's the key. Don't get your hopes up yet, but there may be survivors inside that 747."

"Admiral. I have the commander of the *Cayuga* on the radio. It's Captain Mackenzie, sir."

Corrigan took the microphone. "This is Admiral Corrigan. Do you have a report?"

"Yes, sir," Mackenzie said. "We've been monitoring the rescue channel. We're steaming toward the rescue coordinates and are prepared to take that man on board. We've begun dive preparations, but we'll need additional equipment and more divers."

"Right," Corrigan said. "I'll see that you get what you need. Can you estimate your arrival time?"

"About twenty minutes, sir."

"Captain Mackenzie, will you grant permission for Mr. Stevens to board the *Cayuga*? That's his plane down there."

"Yes, sir, we'll prepare our deck for a helicopter arrival."

"Good," Corrigan said. "And, Captain, you'll be the first ship on the scene. The rescue operation will be your baby. Good luck."

"Roger and out," Mackenzie said.

Corrigan turned. He saw the look of concern on Stevens' face. He placed his hand on the older man's shoulder and spoke reassuringly. "Don't worry, Phil. We're going to get that plane up—and in one piece."

The Navy has had more experience in air-sea rescue than any of the other armed services. Their air-sea rescue branch was organized before the First World War, and they've used their fifty-five years of experience to develop and perfect procedures for the rescue of downed ships and aircraft. When an emergency occurs, this experience has shown them how to respond in an incredibly short period of time. And, as all people in the rescue field know, a few minutes can mean the difference between life and death in an emergency situation.

When the alert horn began to sound at the naval base that adjoined the Tactical Coordination Center, a well-rehearsed procedure was put into effect.

With the horns blasting in their ears, the men at the supplies warehouse sprang into action. Word had come down that this was to be an emergency salvage operation. Warehousemen rushed down aisles of the warehouse in motorized carts. They had well-memorized lists of the kinds of emergency equipment that was needed for different kinds of operations. Each time they stopped, they removed something they needed from a rack and placed it on their cart. It was not unlike a shopping expedition to the most exotic supermarket ever.

Finally, as they finished loading up the different kinds of equipment that was needed—cables, flotation bags, salvage slings, welding equipment, emergency oxygen, and the other oddments that were the diver's stock in trade—they headed their carts for the loading area of the huge warehouse.

Waiting there, by prearrangement, were heavy-duty trucks and a loading crew. The men were ready to move the salvage equipment onto the trucks with speed and efficiency. Then the trucks would head out to the airfield, where huge SH-3 helicopters were awaiting them.

The alert horns were blasting in the barracks, as well. Frogmen who were members of an underwater demolition team rushed from their bunks. Each carried his own scuba equipment, and when the men hopped into the jeeps that were waiting outside to transport them to the airfield, each was completely ready to do his job.

On the landing field, huge SH-3 helicopters spun their

rotors as their turbine engines roared. They were quite warmed up when the trucks of diving equipment arrived.

A loading crew had appeared, and began loading the helicopters with the diving equipment. In only a few minutes the copters were completely loaded and ready to receive the scuba-diving team as it arrived in jeeps.

One final jeep was on its way. It was last, because it had made a stop at the Tactical Coordination Center. In the jeep was Philip Stevens. It pulled up to the last remaining helicopter. Hurriedly Stevens got out and climbed up the ladder into the helicopter. Then, with a clang, the door was slammed shut, and with a scream of accelerating turbines the helicopter rose. It joined the other helicopters, and they headed out to the ocean and the difficult mission that awaited them.

16

Buchek knew that Gallagher had been out of the 747 for only a little more than an hour. But somehow it seemed more like an eternity. He stood by the stairs that led from the main lounge to the flight deck and the upper level of the plane. Water was now cascading down the stairs and darkening the carpet in the main lounge. The volume of water that spilled down the stairs was growing, and Buchek knew that he would have to move the passengers farther forward in the aircraft and get the injured up off the floor. Even so, it was only a matter of time before the main lounge began to fill. He only hoped that rescue would arrive before that occurred.

Buchek moved across the main lounge and looked down the stairs that led to the lower level. Ever since Gallagher had gotten out of the aircraft, the water down below had been rising at a faster and faster rate. Now it was only a few feet from the floor of the main lounge. The main lounge would be filling from two sources. Buchek tried to calculate the speed with which the main lounge would fill. But even if he were able to compute the time they had left, what difference would it make? Their fate was completely in the hands of their rescuers.

St. Downs moved to Buchek. "I think it's time we moved Dorothy."

Buchek nodded in agreement, and the two men moved to where Dorothy was lying on the floor, wrapped in a blanket. Emily Livingston was sitting next to Dorothy and, as the men approached, she got up and began to prepare a sofa. Together the men carefully eased Dorothy off the floor and lifted her onto the sofa.

Dorothy was unconscious, but she moaned slightly in her troubled sleep. Emily sat down on the couch, leaned over her, and patted her fevered forehead with a wet compress. Emily was very concerned. Dorothy's breathing had become quite uneven.

As Buchek moved to help other injured passengers, St. Downs knelt beside Emily. "How does she seem?" he asked.

"Very bad. Oh, Nicky. She's got to live, she's got to!"

St. Downs took Emily's hand in his and pressed it to give her reassurance. But secretly he thought they would all be lucky to live and see another day.

Suddenly, a murmur ran through the groups of passengers. Even Chambers, who had sat alone and depressed ever since Gallagher had told the passengers their situation, stood up and hope crossed his weary face. In the distance was the sound and vibration of an approaching ship. The passengers could scarcely believe their ears. They laughed and cried and hugged each other with the joy of it.

The sound and vibration of the approaching ship increased. This time, the sound didn't die away. As miraculous as it seemed, help was here.

Eve wiped the tears from her eyes. Her heart leaped at the thought that Gallagher was probably safe, and that soon they might be too. He did it, she thought. Don did it! They've finally found us!

The USS *Cayuga* had been involved in a training exercise when the call from Admiral Corrigan had come. Mackenzie had alerted his men to prepare for the mission ahead, and had immediately ordered his ship to proceed to the crash site at full steam.

In the Navy, little time is wasted when an emergency situation exists. All during the time the ship steamed toward the crash site, the sailors on board prepared earnestly for the exceedingly difficult rescue operation that lay ahead. Air compressors, air hoses, oxygen bottles, and almost every imaginable kind of diving paraphernalia they might need was made ready. It was their conscious policy always to overprepare, rather than the opposite, and this was a policy that was proven to save lives.

Mackenzie knew that his ship had been chosen to lead this mission because he had two teams of UDT men on board. The UDT men, which is Navy parlance for underwater-demolition-team members, were already preparing their equipment and stacking it on deck. They were all crack divers and were fully experienced both in scuba diving and in the salvage and recovery of sunken vessels. Now, as the *Cayuga* headed toward the crash site, they were gathered on the deck, making the checks and rechecks on their equipment that would help ensure their safety in the water. They relied totally on their equipment, because it was the one insurance they had in a job that was, at best, terribly risky.

Captain Mackenzie was a short, stocky man in his early forties. He stood on the bridge of the *Cayuga* readying himself for the rescue operation that was soon to come. He looked out of the windows of the bridge and saw that the helicopter pads on the quarterdeck had been cleared. Two semaphore men were already in position to guide in the helicopters that would be arriving with additional divers, rescue equipment, and Mr. Stevens, the owner of the downed plane.

The intership communicator whistled. He picked it up.

"I have contact, sir. One-zero-eight degrees starboard. Man in life raft, sir."

Mackenzie snapped off the communicator and raised his binoculars to his eyes. Suddenly he spotted the tiny life raft bobbing in the water with its human cargo. Mackenzie turned to his first officer. "All engines half. Right rudder eighty-five degrees. Let's prepare to get that man on board and start our salvage operation!"

With mounting anticipation, Gallagher had watched the small speck on the horizon of the ocean grow larger and larger. He didn't know that it was a Navy rescue ship, but it was a ship, and that was good enough. Gallagher waited in the life raft, shivering with cold. He had never known such frustration, for until help arrived there was nothing he could do for the passengers trapped in the 747 down below.

But once the *Cayuga* came into sight, Gallagher was amazed at the speed with which things happened. Even before the large ship had dropped anchor, a "zodiac," a large rubber boat powered by an outboard motor, was lowered into the ocean from the *Cayuga*. The rubber boat was manned by members of the Navy UDT team, dressed in wet suits. It cut a swath in the water as it sped out to Gallagher, managing the choppy water with no difficulty. It drew alongside Gallagher's life raft, and the crew members helped Gallagher into the zodiac, then sped back to the mother ship.

A medical corpsman checked Gallagher quickly in the zodiac. Then he helped Gallagher wrap himself in a heavy wool blanket. Another crewman passed Gallagher a cup of steaming coffee he'd drawn from a thermos. After Gallagher had taken a few long pulls on the warming coffee, the medical corpsman asked him if he felt better.

"I'm fine," Gallagher said. "It's those people who are trapped in the plane that need help. We've got to get them out fast."

A tall, laconic UDT man named Lawson turned to Gallagher. He pointed to the UDT symbol of a dolphin that was inscribed on his wet suit. "That's what we're here for, Captain," he said.

The zodiac arrived at the gangway of the *Cayuga*, and Gallagher was helped out of the boat. He hurried up the gangway as fast as he could. He knew that he had vital information that the commander of the operation would need before any rescue attempt could begin.

On the main deck, Gallagher was met by the officer of the day. He told the man who he was, and the O.D. escorted him to the bridge. As Gallagher hurried along, he noticed that rescue preparations were being made all

170

around him. He saw UDT team members transferring their scuba tanks to waiting zodiacs; in another area, air hoses and high-pressure pumps were being readied. Elsewhere, crewmen were taking the canvas tops from UDT boats and were securing winches to lower them over the side. All that he saw gave Gallagher the first feeling of hope he'd had for a long time.

On the bridge, Captain Mackenzie approached Gallagher and the O.D. The O.D. saluted Mackenzie. "Captain, this is Mr. Gallagher, captain of the downed aircraft."

Mackenzie shook hands with Gallagher. "What's the situation down there?"

"Most of the passengers are alive. Many are injured, some badly. But the fuselage is starting to give way. I don't know how much water's in that plane by now."

"How's the air?" Mackenzie asked.

"Not good," Gallagher said. "They've been down there a long time. When can you start rescue operations?"

In the background, Mackenzie could hear the sound of approaching jet turbines and the chop of rotor blades in the air. He motioned toward the sounds. "There's your answer, Captain Gallagher," he said.

Fast approaching the USS *Cayuga* were three large SH-3 naval transport helicopters. They came close to the *Cayuga*, then hovered over the ocean like large insects. The copters had brought their payload of equipment and UDT men from the Jacksonville Tactical Coordination Center.

"Come with me," Mackenzie said, and he led Gallagher out of the bridge and down toward the helicopter pads on the quarterdeck.

A helicopter moved away from the ocean and over the helicopter pad on the *Cayuga*. The wind and noisy turbulence that its rotors caused were incredible, but no more incredible than the pinpoint landing the helicopter was able to achieve. Even though the ship rolled and tossed in the heavy seas, and the helicopter pad was barely

171

larger than the aircraft itself, the Navy semaphore man was able to guide it to a safe landing that looked deceptively easy.

Gallagher and Captain Mackenzie reached the quarterdeck in time to see the helicopter touch down. Instantly the UDT men inside hopped to the deck. Their equipment was handed to them by the helicopter crewmen, and ducking to avoid the whirling blade, they hurried off the helicopter pad. As soon as they were clear, the helicopter lifted off again and hovered alongside the ship. Its place was immediately taken by the next helicopter, whose crew and equipment were unloaded with the same speed and efficiency as before.

The same well-organized chaos on the helicopter pad continued during the unloading of the third helicopter.

The entire unloading operation seemed to be under the supervision of Lieutenant Lawson, the tall laconic frogman who had spoken to Gallagher earlier. Lawson would lead the team of scuba divers that would swim underwater to the 747. He was talking with his Jacksonville counterpart, Lieutenant Carrothers. Lawson was quickly filling him in on the situation and the proposed plan of attack they would use to attempt the rescue of the passengers in the downed 747. Carrothers nodded his agreement, saluted Captain Mackenzie, then went to join his men.

As the last of the men got out of the third helicopter, Gallagher saw a familiar face. Philip Stevens was among the men climbing out of the helicopter. Stevens quickly moved to Gallagher and warmly shook his hand. Immediately Gallagher told him that most of the guests were alive, and that his daughter and grandson were among the uninjured. He also told him how the plane had crashed, and who was responsible. There was a look of noticeable relief on Philip Stevens' face, but then the thought of all the others and their desperate plight below returned the look of worry to his craggy features.

Mackenzie led Gallagher and Stevens away from the noise of the helo pad. They walked forward on the ship to

172

where Lieutenant Lawson and his UDT team were waiting. Lawson left his men and crossed to Mackenzie. "Sir, we're ready to begin, at your order."

Stevens turned to Mackenzie. "Captain, just what is it that you plan to do?"

"If there were only a few people on that plane, Mr. Stevens, we'd have no problem. We'd cut into the skin of the aircraft and get scuba divers inside with extra oxygen bottles for the passengers. Then we'd bring the passengers out, one at a time. That's impossible in this case. There are far too many people inside there to bring them out individually. Some are too badly injured to survive, and others would drown before we got to them."

"Then how is it possible to save them?" Stevens asked.

"We're going to raise that plane, Mr. Stevens. We'll use inflatable lifting bags. The same kind we use to raise sunken ships. Lieutenant Lawson here will lead the UDT team that will place the bags."

Gallagher stepped forward and faced Mackenzie. "I'm going with them."

"Are you a diver?" Mackenzie asked skeptically.

"Amateur."

Mackenzie shook his head. "No way, Mr. Gallagher. I can't permit that."

As though that ended the conversation, Mackenzie turned to Lawson. But Gallagher wouldn't be put off that easily. He had been under tremendous strain for the past eighteen hours, and his temper was very short.

"Captain, your men don't know the stress points on a 747. I do. Attach one of those salvage bags in the wrong place, and you'll crack that plane wide open."

As his anger built, Gallagher's voice got progressively louder. Several of the crew members who were nearby watched with unbelieving eyes. In the U.S. Navy, you don't yell at the captain of a ship. Mackenzie said nothing. He listened as Gallagher spoke, and regarded him coldly.

"Those people have been through too much to have their last chance taken away," Gallagher said. "Goddammit! You need me down there!"

The nearby crew members waited for Mackenzie to explode. They knew Mackenzie had a short temper himself and that at any moment he might lose that temper.

Instead, Mackenzie thought about what Gallagher had said for a moment, then smiled benignly. "I admire your persistence, Captain Gallagher. I think that if you hadn't gone into aviation, you might have made a pretty good naval officer." Mackenzie turned to Lawson. "What are you waiting for? Get this man into some scuba gear. On the double."

Water poured down the stairs from the upper level of the 747. Its volume of flow increased with each passing minute. The water in the main lounge was now more than knee-deep.

Buchek saw that it would soon be impossible to keep Dorothy and the other injured people out of the water, which was continually rising. Still, he thought, he could make them as comfortable as possible. He motioned to St. Downs to follow him, and the two men waded through the knee-deep water as they moved to the rear portion of the main lounge.

Buchek went to the bin that contained life jackets and began taking armloads of the jackets out. St. Downs did the same, then they moved to rejoin the guests. Buchek called to the guests, who huddled together, shivering with wet and cold, thoroughly terrified.

"Let's get these life jackets on the injured. As the water rises, it'll keep their heads above it."

Buchek moved among the guests, passing out the jackets and whispering words of encouragement. There was an atmosphere of total gloom in the lounge. Although rescue was at hand, few of the guests felt anything could be done before the lounge filled completely with water. It would be the final ironic joke, for them all to die with their rescuers just outside.

Although Buchek felt much the same way as the passengers did, he tried his best not to show it.

"Listen to me, everyone. After you get the life jackets on the injured, put them on yourselves. When the rescue starts, we'll need the jackets, so we might as well put them on now."

The stewardesses showed the guests how the jackets worked, and everyone began putting the jackets on. Somehow, having something to do, no matter how simple, seemed to cheer the passengers up. Buchek moved to Mrs. Stern and helped her slip a life jacket on Bonnie. As he moved through the water toward her, he noticed that it was already perceptibly higher than it had been a few minutes ago.

17

The two scuba teams headed toward the crash site in rubber zodiac boats. Their high-powered outboard motors made them skip along the tops of the heavy waves as they went. The men were dressed in wet suits and were wearing scuba tanks, masks, and flippers. Gallagher and Lawson, the man in charge of the scuba teams, rode in the first zodiac. As they approached the site where the 747 was underwater, Lawson questioned Gallagher, trying to get as much information as he could before they went underwater.

With pencil and paper Gallagher had drawn a simple sketch of the 747. As he talked, he marked off the areas that he thought would be potential trouble spots.

"The worst fuselage damage is in the forward cargo hold," Gallagher said, as he indicated the location on the diagram he had drawn.

"We'll check that out first. Can we risk getting air to the passengers?"

Gallagher shook his head. "It's too risky. Start cutting into that thin aluminum, and who knows what will happen."

Lawson nodded agreement. He moved a coil of hose and retrieved a small slate board that had a piece of oily chalk attached to it with a piece of string. "We'll use this to let the passengers inside the plane know what we're going to do. How well organized are they? What's the chance of a panic?"

Gallagher thought of Buchek and Eve, both of whom he had complete faith in. "Don't worry. You won't have any problems with that."

Gallagher looked back over the rough ocean to the *Cayuga*. He saw that large LCVP boats were being lowered over the side by the *Cayuga*'s cargo cranes. The designation LCVP stood for "Landing Craft Vehicle Personnel." The tough little steel boats could carry a dozen people, or five tons of equipment with little difficulty. Only now, manned by the *Cayuga*'s trained crews, they were loaded with the equipment that would be used in the attempt to raise the plane. Gallagher watched as the last LCVP plopped into the water. He knew that by the time he, Lawson and the survey team finished their work, the equipment needed for raising the 747 would be in place.

The zodiac boats slowed as they reached the location under which was the 747.

Lawson shouted to his men as the zodiacs came to a full stop. "Gentlemen, we have our instructions. Let's do it!" Lawson slipped his mask into place, and followed by Gallagher, rolled over the side of the zodiac boat and disappeared beneath the surface of the water. One by one, the other members of the scuba teams followed suit.

Gallagher felt the initial cold shock of the water as he slipped beneath the waves. Then, his wet suit filled and the thin film of water between him and the suit warmed and insulated his body from the chill of the ocean. He adjusted his mask, breathed deeply from his air supply, and propelled himself with his flippers down into the depths.

Gallagher swam next to Lawson, and as they went deeper in the murky green water, the huge plane became visible ahead of them. It seemed so huge, resting on the ocean floor, that Gallagher felt insignificant in comparison. The windows of the plane looked like a row of dim yellow eyes, silhouetted against which were the figures of the passengers. Somehow, Gallagher thought, it was more like some prehistoric leviathan than a manmade object of steel and aluminum.

The men dived deeper and approached the monstrous aircraft. The crews split into different groups at this point, some going to the forward cargo areas, others to the rear, others examining the plane's huge wings. But Gallagher and Lawson went directly to the windows of the plane. A direct examination of the passenger area was necessary so that they could immediately make an evaluation of the possibilities for rescue.

Inside the main lounge, there was general rejoicing. The passengers had seen the scuba teams heading down through the water toward the plane. It was the first concrete example they had seen that help was at hand. It wasn't a goddamn minute too soon, thought Buchek. The water that was cascading down the stairs from the upper level of the plane into the main lounge had tripled in volume in the last few minutes. The water was now approaching waist height, and Buchek was sure the lounge would fill completely within the hour.

Shivering with cold, Buchek had inflated the life jacket that was around Dorothy's neck. Since there was no longer any dry place for her to lie, the inflated life vest would at least keep her head out of the water. The same thing was done for Eddie, although he had been managing to stand on his one good leg. As the water rose, the temperature in the main lounge fell, and all the passengers were experiencing the effects of the cold water they were standing in.

But now that help was here, the passengers were able to forget their cold discomfort as they flocked to see the divers outside the windows of the main lounge.

Buchek moved to a window and looked out. He saw that one of the divers had an underwater slate board and that he was writing on it with a piece of chalk. Buchek pushed his way through a group of passengers and moved to the window closest to the diver. The diver finished writing and held up the slate board. It read, "WILL RAISE PLANE, SECURE ALL." Buchek gave the diver the A-OK sign and turned to the passengers. "They're going to try to bring the plane to the surface. When they do, it'll be like a hurricane hit us. Let's station ourselves where we can hold on. Find anything solid and grab on to it. Use your belts. Make sure the injured are secure." He moved among the passengers, helping them find areas where they would be relatively safe as the plane was raised. "Listen, some of you should use torn-up strips of blanket if you don't have belts." He looked toward the front of the main lounge. "Tie yourselves to that stair railing. It should be secure." The guests moved to comply, and Buchek went to help Emily and St. Downs with the injured Dorothy.

Gallagher had caught a glimpse of Eve Clayton inside the main lounge. Like the rest of the passengers, there was fear on her face, but now there was also hope. The fact that the water inside the main lounge was rising so fast was frightening to Gallagher. He only hoped that they had enough time to do what was necessary. Lawson turned to him and pointed down toward the forward cargo hold. Gallagher gestured that he understood, and he quickly swam to join Lawson. Together the two men swam the length of the plane toward the hold.

Ahead of them was the torn metal of the plane's skin. This was where the cargo container had smashed through the plane's skin during the crash. If it hadn't been for this large tear in the fuselage, the plane would probably have retained enough buoyancy to stay afloat long enough for the passengers to get out. As it was, with a hole this size in the cargo area, the plane had gone down like a stone.

Lawson pulled a high-intensity flashlight from his belt and snapped it on. They were joined by two other frogmen, who grabbed hold of the torn metal and pulled it aside. Then Gallagher and the other frogmen glided into the cargo compartment of the plane.

An incredible amount of debris from the crash floated in and out of the flashlight beam. The beam played over the ruined paintings, the destroyed sculptures. Then it illuminated a sight that made even the experienced frogmen jolt. It was a face, bloated and hideous from the long hours spent in the water. It was Banker, and his body was still pinned by the aluminum cargo container.

Gallagher directed Lawson to move the beam over to the left. The beam played across the bulkhead, then stopped at the spot Gallagher was searching for. It was the door that led from the cargo hold to the interior of the plane. The door seal was still holding, but not very well. Bubbles were coming from the side of the seal. Gallagher and Lawson swam close and examined the seal. Lawson motioned to members of his crew. They would immediately begin securing a patch to the area. That would help, but would it hold under the jarring impact of the plane being raised? If the door went, the plane would flood instantly, drowning all the passengers. But they would have to risk it.

Lawson motioned to Gallagher, and the two men made their way out of the cargo hold and outside the plane.

Now began a process that would take a great deal of time, but was of the utmost importance. The plane would be raised with lifting bags. These were the most recent technological development in marine salvage. The lifting bags were huge rubber bags that would be strapped to various parts of the plane. The bags would then be inflated with air. Their combined lifting power was tremendous. They had been designed for lifting ships, which were far heavier than the 747, and consequently the bags had so much lifting power that it was feared they might tear the 747 apart if they were attached at a point where the metal was weak or the structure was unsound. The diving team, now led by Gallagher, would check every part of the plane's exterior. Gallagher would point out the places at which the large lifting bags could be attached with a minimum of risk.

After rejecting two spots at the rear of the plane, Gallagher finally settled on two locations near the tail of the plane. Then they found four points where the huge wings of the 747 met the fuselage. In each spot, a frogman with waterproof chalk marked a huge X for the team that would be attaching the lifting bags and the air hoses that would inflate them.

The work went agonizingly slowly. As Gallagher

carefully supervised the choosing of the locations for the lifting bags, he could not free his mind of the sight he had seen through the windows of the main lounge. The water was rapidly filling the lounge, and he could not shake from his memory the frightened and pleading faces that had watched him from the windows of the aircraft.

Finally the work was done. At least, Gallagher thought, the bags will be attached where they'll do the least damage to the structure of the plane. If it held together, there was a good chance they would get the plane to the surface.

Lawson motioned to Gallagher and the other divers. Quickly they began their ascent to the surface of the ocean and the second phase of the rescue plan.

While the scuba team was underwater surveying the damage to the 747 and determining where the lifting bags would be attached to the huge plane, a great deal of activity was occurring on the surface of the water.

A huge air hose had been connected to one of the *Cayuga*'s air compressors. It ran up the stairs from the engine room, over the quarterdeck, then over the side of the ship into the ocean. LCVP boats were towing the air hose out to the area above the sunken 747, adding sections to the hose as they went.

When the hose reached the crash site, it was connected to a salvage manifold in one of the LCVPs. Basically, the salvage manifold was a console that contained many different hose connections and pressure regulators. The main air line was connected to it; then a number of feeder hoses would go from the manifold and be stretched by divers down to the 747 that rested on the bottom.

Another LCVP carried the lifting bags. The bags were made of rubber, were painted orange, and lay neatly folded in the LCVP. Each had an air-hose connection, and when it was inflated, would become more than ten feet in diameter and have the lifting power to raise many tons of weight.

Lawson, Gallagher, and the rest of the scuba team broke the surface of the water. Instantly, crewmen were moving to them in rubber zodiac boats. The crewmen, with practiced efficiency, gave the scuba-team members the tools and equipment they would need for the job ahead. Each man snapped on a utility belt, containing tools and specialized salvage equipment. Then the scuba team broke off into small groups, each group heading for a different LCVP, which in the meantime had drawn closer to them.

One group of scuba divers was handed the lifting bags. The heavy rubber bags had built-in carrying handles, and it took two men to carry each bag. As they received their lifting bags, the groups of divers disappeared beneath the surface of the water.

At another LCVP, a group of divers was receiving the air hoses that would be attached to the lifting bags underwater.

A third team, including Gallagher and Lawson, received the harness and special couplings that would attach the lifting bags to the fuselage of the 747.

Each team got what it needed, then slipped under the surface of the water, rushing against time to try to complete the work before it was too late.

As Gallagher swam alongside Lawson, he was amazed at the almost balletic precision and teamwork the three diving crews displayed. They swam straight toward one of the huge wings of the aircraft. They would start there. One of the team members unsnapped a compressed-air gun from his belt and stationed himself at the large X that they had earlier scrawled on the wing with chalk. Gallagher indicated an area that was well away from the fuselage, and the team member fired a bolt directly into the wing of the plane. He moved twelve feet over and fired another bolt into the wing's forward edge. Now there were two points where air bags could be attached.

Gallagher's team moved away, toward the tail of the plane. They would repeat this bolt-setting operation at each point on the plane where a lifting bag was to be connected.

As Gallagher's team swam toward the rear of the

plane, a second team of frogmen approached the mounting bolts that had been attached to the wings. This group of frogmen carried the air bags. The bags waved in the ocean current like lazy yellow jellyfish. Two frogmen floated the cumbersome bags over to the metal bolts. They attached a bag to the bolts by snap couplers and lenths of steel cable that were fixed to the bottom of the bag. Then they kicked away from the wing and headed toward the tail of the plane, to repeat the operation there.

In a few seconds, the third team of divers arrived. They carried with them the long air hoses that were connected to the manifold on the surface of the ocean. The weight of the hose was considerable, and it weaved and bobbed behind them in a snakelike undulation as they pulled it toward the lifting bag that was attached to the wing. Together, two men brought the mouth of the hose to a coupling on the lifting bag. A third frogman unsnapped a wrench from his utility belt and tightly screwed the hose to the coupling on the bag. When the coupling was tightly on, the men checked all the connections that held the lifting bag. At the other mounting points on the aircraft, the same operations were being carried out.

When Gallagher finally returned to the surface of the ocean, he was exhausted. He swam to the lead zodiac boat and was helped in by a crew member. Behind him, Lawson's head popped out of the water, and soon Lawson was also in the zodiac.

Lawson reached for the walkie-talkie unit. He extended its antenna, then pressed the communicator button. "Captain Mackenzie? This is Lawson."

Mackenzie's voice emerged from the walkie-talkie, loud and clear. "How is it, Lawson?"

"That plane's leaking like a sieve. I don't think we should wait much longer before we raise her."

"What about the weight distribution?" Mackenzie asked.

"The plane's tail-heavy. It's going to come up at a steep angle."

"Is there time to equalize the load or add more lifting bags?"

"No, sir." Lawson said. "I don't want to risk taking the time."

"Then move those boats back," Mackenzie said. "I'm starting the compressors. We're going to have to chance it."

The motors of the zodiacs and LCVPs were all idling smoothly. Gallagher looked around and saw that, one by one, the scuba teams were coming to the surface. He helped the rest of his team into the zodiac, as did the men on the other zodiacs. The boats all began to move back toward the *Cayuga*.

For better or worse, they were going to try to lift the plane to the surface.

Hank Buchek took a strip of torn sheet and carefully tied it around Eddie's waist. The injured man was holding on to the railing of the stairs that led to the upper deck. Water poured down the stairs, and his position was extremely uncomfortable, but the railing was solid and was the best place that Buchek could find for the man. After he had wrapped the strip of sheet around Eddie's waist, Buchek secured it to the stair railing.

"That's pretty tight, Mr. Buchek," Eddie said, wincing.

"I'm sorry, Eddie. But it's got to be that way," Buchek said. He finished tying the sheet and turned to Emily Livingston and Nicholas St. Downs. They stood against the stair railing, next to Eddie, holding Dorothy between them. Strips of sheet held Dorothy against the stairs in a standing position. Dorothy worried Buchek. She was in no condition to be kept standing up. Her breathing was very shallow now, and it was obvious she was in terribly serious condition. But equally obvious was the fact that nothing could be done for her.

Buchek helped Mrs. Stern, who was holding Bonnie, take a position at the railing. He helped them secure themselves, then moved to check the rest of the passengers.

A few feet forward of the stairs, there was a waist-high partition on each side of the main lounge. A built-in table at each partition provided a secure handhold. Lisa and Benjy were tied with sheets to one partition. On the opposite side of the lounge, Karen Wallace had tied herself to the other.

Buchek checked all of the passengers, making sure each of them was secure. After making certain that the others were all right, he moved to the stairs and tied himself in place. He knew that they wouldn't have long to wait.

18

Captain Mackenzie stood on the bridge of the *Cayuga*. Next to him stood Philip Stevens. Behind them, a number of ship's crewmen and officers tensely waited for orders.

Mackenzie wateched the rescue site through binoculars. He saw the small boats withdraw from the rescue area and saw the LCVP that contained the manifold stop in position. Mackenzie turned to a lieutenant. "The boats have pulled back a safe distance. We can start the compressor."

The lieutenant put on a headset and spoke directly to the compressor crew. Immediately, the clacking sound of reciprocal pistons was heard. The operation had started.

On the main deck, the compressor chattered away. A chief mate watched the pressure gauge rise as pressure built up in the accumulator tank. When the proper amount of pressure had built up, the chief gravely signaled to one of his men, and the pressure valve was opened.

There was a scream of air pressure as the hose filled and then went rigid on the deck. The hose moved and thrashed as the high-pressure air stream moved through it.

The air filled the line, moving through foot after foot of air hose until it reached the manifold in the LCVP boat that was waiting just off the site of the sunken 747.

In the LCVP the salvage officer watched the gauge on the manifold and waited for it to reach full pressure. The manifold would feed air to the air bags that had been attached to the sunken plane. Finally, the main line had brought the pressure up full, and the diving officer signaled to his men.

Quickly, all the valves that fed the air bags were opened. The bags would fill at once, and if everything went well, their buoyancy would soon begin bringing the 747 to the surface.

Six air bags were attached to the 747. Four were attached to the wing, close to the fuselage on either side. Two were mounted on the tail section, one on each side. The lifting power of these bags, when inflated, would be tremendous.

Now the long hoses that reached from the bags to the surface of the ocean became rigid as the air destined for the bags coursed through them. The limp bags began to sway and shift as air pressure began to surge into them. Pressure valves on the bags ensured the steadiness of the air flow and vented huge quantities of bubbles into the water. As the bags filled, the ocean and the sandy bottom beneath the plane shifted and moved in great turmoil. The bags, as they filled, changed shape and enlarged. They were transformed from yellow pennants that undulated in the currents into giant spheres more than ten feet in diameter. Still, they kept filling and enlarging, the air pressure inside them displacing the weight of the 747 little by little. As the bags filled, they swayed and rocked, pulling against the mounting bolts that held them to the 747. The metal of the aircraft protested as the bags jerked against it, time and time again. With each jerk of the bags, there was a sound of impact that echoed through the water.

The plane suddenly began to shift position. There was a groaning sound from the metal of the plane, almost as if it were a live thing that was being torn apart at its joints by giant stresses.

The 747 was held to the bottom of the ocean with considerable suction. As the plane shifted position and moved, huge clouds of sand and silt were displaced. The

747 shifted away from the bottom, then slammed back down again several times.

All the while, the air bags kept filling and filling with air, growing stronger with every moment as the air inside them displaced the weight of the 747.

The tension on the *Cayuga* was incredible. The men stood at the rail, silent, waiting and hoping as they looked toward the spot where the 747 would emerge. Only the relentless sound of the air compressor cut the silence.

On the bridge, Mackenzie stood watching the ocean through binoculars. The sea was boiling as released air pressure made the water roll and churn. When he saw the boiling water begin to turn sandy brown, he knew that the bags were beginning to lift the 747 from the bottom. Mackenzie was extremely concerned. If only they had had more time! He knew that the four bags attached to the forward part of the aircraft would make the plane rise out-of-balance. The nose would rise much faster than the tail, and the plane would come up like a bullet. Mackenzie hoped that the passengers inside were well secured. It would be hell inside that aircraft as it rose to the surface.

The vibrations and tremors that shook the 747 seemed to be magnified inside the main lounge. Each time an air bag pulled against its mounting bolt, the entire aircraft seemed to pitch and threaten to throw the passengers from their feet. The sound of groaning metal was terrifying, and at any moment the passengers expected the 747 to split apart.

The passengers held on to the partitions and the stairwell with every particle of strength they had. Buchek, who was in front of the stairwell, clutching the railing, cursed that he had only one good hand, because Eve Clayton, who held on next to him, was getting seriously battered around by the motion of the plane.

Suddenly the movement of the plane became violent, and it began to rock from side to side. The waist-high water began moving from one side to the other in waves.

Little Bonnie Stern wailed in terror and coughed as water splashed over her head. Then, the angle of the floor began to change under their feet. There was a surge in the movement of the water, and Buchek saw that it was suddenly getting deeper as water rushed from the forward part of the plane to the rear. As the angle of the floor grew steeper, Buchek knew that the plane was beginning to rise.

He felt the floor begin to slip out from beneath him, and he had to grip the stairwell railing more tightly. As the angle of the floor increased, Buchek, to his horror, realized what was wrong. The plane was going to go to the surface at a steep angle. He shouted to the others to hold on, it was going to be rough. There were screams of terror as the angle of the floor increased and huge volumes of water came pouring past them from the forward part of the plane. Soon they were being peppered with debris of all sorts as it was carried past them on its way to the rear of the plane. Buchek looked around and tried to see all the other passengers. Most seemed well secured. However, just forward of the stairwell, Lisa and Benjy held on to a partition, and just opposite them, on the other side of the main lounge, Karen Wallace held on to an identical partition. Buchek realized that if the plane rolled at all from side to side, those people would be in grave danger.

The plane rocked and shook violently as it made its way to the surface of the water. The angle of the plane was so steep now that the inside of the main lounge was like a greased playground slide. Anything that wasn't firmly tied down was rolling and tumbling to the rear of the main lounge and into the corridor that led to the rear of the plane.

Behind the stairwell, the passengers hung on to the railing, being battered by the water that rushed past them in huge waves. Chambers held onto the stairwell with all his strength, his eyes wild with panic and fear. Eddie screamed as his injured leg was banged against the stairwell. Next to him, St. Downs and Emily did their best to protect Dorothy with their own bodies.

Buchek heard a ripping and tearing sound from the front of the plane and then watched in horror as a chair, swept along by the flood, crashed into Dr. Williams from behind, hitting him between the shoulderblades. Williams let out a cry of pain but managed to keep his hold on the stair railing. The chair bounced off the wall, barely missed hitting Lisa and Benjy, and then was swept down the main lounge and disappeared in the corridor leading to the rear of the plane. Buchek tried desperately to hold on to the slippery railing. He knew that if the plane didn't level out soon, they'd all, ultimately, be swept away in the rushing water.

Ralph Crawford felt his hands slipping from the slick railing. Frantically he tried to readjust his grip, but at that moment the aircraft rolled to the side and back again. Losing his balance, he felt his handhold slipping away. He gulped down seawater, felt his mouth and nose burning from it. Desperately he clutched at anything he could, but his hands grabbed only seawater. He felt himself begin to fall, tumbling as though he were in a nightmare. Then, his hand was suddenly grasped in a firm grip. With his other hand Crawford flailed in the water, then grasped the wrist of the man who was holding him. Gripping as hard as he could, Crawford brought his head above the furious water. He could see that it was Lucas who was straining as hard as he could to hold on to him. Lucas had one arm wrapped around the stair railing, and with all his might he was pulling on Crawford's arm. With a last desperate effort from his exhausted body, Crawford pulled himself forward and grabbed the stair railing. Then, without an ounce of strength left in him, he wrapped his arms around the railing, breathing in jagged gasps.

Thank God, thought Buchek. He could see that Crawford, though frightened out of his wits, was all right. But Buchek knew that Crawford had been lucky. The incline of the floor was steadily increasing. Furniture and debris were being hurled like missiles to the back of the lounge. If they didn't reach the surface of the water soon,

Buchek knew that some of the passengers would inevitably be swept to their deaths in the rear portion of the plane.

From their position in the zodiac boat, Gallagher and Lawson watched the turmoil on the ocean where the 747 would break the surface. The entire area, about fifty square yards, was a boiling caldron of churning water and bubbles from the tremendous disturbance that was taking place below.

The area was ringed with zodiac boats, which were filled with frogmen, anxiously awaiting the last and most hazardous part of the operation. Their zodiac boats were as close as was possible to the area where the plane would break the surface. They would have to get the survivors off that airplane as swiftly as they could.

Using binoculars, Lawson watched the area intently. As the turmoil intensified, he could tell that the plane was nearing the surface. He put down the binoculars and turned to Gallagher. "This is one baby we're going to have to crack as fast as we can. With those balloons positioned as they are, we've got a very unstable condition. That plane could go down as fast as it's coming up. And if it does go down again, it's going to take everything nearby with it!"

Lawson checked the surface of the water with his binoculars again. Then he put them down, stood up in the zodiac, and waved his arm toward the other zodiac boats. It was the signal the men had been waiting for. The plane would break the surface any second now. The operation was about to begin.

Gallagher and Lawson slipped on their air masks and adjusted their regulators.

Inside the main lounge of the 747, the passengers were attempting to hold on and fight against the force of the rushing water in the plane and the debris that hurtled by.

Benjy and Lisa were desperately clutching at the partition. There was little to hold on to, and they felt

192

extremely vulnerable as debris crashed past their handholds. Suddenly the plane rolled to one side. Although Lisa was holding Benjy as hard as she could, she could feel him slipping out of her grasp. Lisa had to use one hand to maintain her balance. She was horrified to discover that Benjy was slowly but surely slipping out of the other.

The little boy screamed in terror as he felt his body slipping away from the partition and into the raging river of water that sped to the rear of the plane. He held on to his mother's arm, but little by little he was being carried farther out into the center of the plane, where the force of the water was the strongest.

Lisa, still holding on to the partition with one hand, desperately held Benjy's hand with the other. She looked across to the other partition, which Karen Wallace clung to. She realized that Karen could reach out with one arm and grab the little boy. She screamed at Karen. "Help me! For God's sake, help me!"

Unbelieving, Lisa watched as Karen looked toward Benjy, then withdrew, averting her eyes from Lisa. Instead of reaching out for the little boy, Karen grabbed the partition even tighter.

Buchek held to the stairwell, watching in horror as the little boy slipped farther and farther out into the mainstream of the water. With only one good arm, Buchek felt rage that he couldn't do something to help the child. Suddenly an idea hit him. He turned to Frank Powers, who clung to the railing next to him. "Grab my belt. Hold on to me! I'm going to reach for the kid!"

Powers nodded understanding. He looped one arm around the stair railing, then grasped the back of Buchek's belt, holding it as tightly as he could and bracing himself with all his force.

Now Buchek let go of the stair railing and leaned forward as Powers took his full weight. With his good arm, Buchek reached forward. Water continually splashed over his head, and he could barely see what he was doing. Finally his hand found the collar of the little boy's shirt. Buchek grabbed, pulling Benjy to him. Painfully, against the flow of the water, Buchek used his strength to bring the boy closer and closer. Finally Benjy was close enough to wrap his arms around Buchek's neck.

Powers pulled on Buchek's belt with all his strength. At last Buchek was close enough to the stair railing to grab it again with his good arm. Powers and Buchek both held Benjy, and Lisa gasped with relief when she realized that her son was safe.

The metal of the plane protested and groaned as the aircraft continued to rise to the surface. Suddenly the plane rolled again, tilting to the other side. Abruptly, Karen Wallace felt herself slipping from behind her partition. Her hands slipped along the partition as the plane rolled more and more to one side. Screaming in horror, she finally lost her grip and slipped into the maelstrom of water and debris.

The passengers looked on, helpless, as Karen was carried away by the water. The raging river carried her quickly toward the back of the aircraft. Her screams continued as she was carried to the back of the main lounge. Abruptly, her screams stopped as she was struck by a huge chunk of debris. Her body disappeared, swept down the corridor that led to the back portion of the 747.

The turmoil on the surface of the water grew as the 747 came closer and closer to daylight. Even though most of the diving teams' zodiac boats were stationed many yards from where the plane would surface, the small boats bobbed and rocked violently in the expanding turbulence created by the 747.

Then, with an incredible roar, the bright orange tops of the inflated lifting bags became visible. They were immediately followed by the bright aluminum nose of the 747. Finally, with tons of seawater falling from it, the rest of the 747 roared upward through the rolling waves of the ocean. Glinting in the sun, the aircraft came up as if it were a surfacing whale, and came to rest on the surface, supported, however temporarily, by the lifting bags and the surface of the water.

The waves created by the emergence of the 747 struck against the sides of the zodiac boats. Lawson gave the signal, and the boats sped toward the 747 at full speed.

The gigantic wings of the plane were at surface level. They smacked the ocean as the plane rocked back and forth in the lulling rhythm of the sea.

Lawson, in the lead zodiac, guided the craft toward the wing of the plane. One emergency-exit door was just over the wing, and they could most effectively get the passengers from the plane to their boats through this exit. Lawson was very concerned. They'd have to hurry on this one. The plane's instability in the water and the lack of an adequate number of lifting bags meant that the plane could go back down at any time.

The plane shook and rolled as it came to the surface. Suddenly, sunlight flooded through the windows of the main lounge. It seemed so bright to the passengers, who had spent the past eight hours in a twilight dimness, that they painfully blinked their eyes.

For a second there was silence, for they could hardly believe they were no longer trapped beneath the water. Then the first shout of joy, from Jane Stern, sounded in the aircraft, and then the sounds of relief and cries of happiness filled the lounge.

People quickly untied themselves and then helped the injured get untied.

Buchek turned to them. "Hurry, we've got very little time. Let's get the injured to the center emergency exit. We'll get them out first; then the rest of us will follow. Come on—"

Buchek moved to Eddie and helped the injured man toward the door. Eve Clayton took one of Eddie's arms, and the two of them managed to help Eddie across the now slippery floor.

At the stairs, Nicholas St. Downs held Emily

Livingston in a silent embrace. Dorothy's head rested against Emily's shoulder. Emily turned and hugged Dorothy.

"We're safe, darling. You're going to be all right."

But there was no response. Dorothy's head slumped to one side. Her eyes were closed, and there was no sign of pulse or breath. With a shock, Emily realized that her old friend was dead. It was unbearable. Tears welled up in her eyes, and she began to sob. Nicholas St. Downs put his arms around Emily, trying to console her. "Come," he said, "there's nothing we can do for her now, Emily."

"Oh, Nicky," Emily said. "We can't just leave her here."

"There's no time," St. Downs said gently. It was true. Already, the passengers were at the emergency door, with Buchek and Eve Clayton in charge of the evacuation. They were getting the injured ready and preparing to open the emergency door.

Buchek threw the handle on the door to the open position. The door opened slightly inward, then Buchek pushed it outward. The door sprang open. Immediately, the chill fresh air flooded into the stale, fear-filled atmosphere of the plane. It smelled delicious. Outside, the guests could see the choppy sea and the naval rescue vessels waiting for them.

As frogmen clambered up the wing of the plane and came close to the emergency exit, the passengers made ready to begin helping the injured out of the plane.

Captain Mackenzie and Philip Stevens watched the rescue through binoculars from the bridge of the USS *Cayuga*.

It was amazing how tiny the zodiac boats seemed next to the huge 747. Even the large SH-3 helicopters that hovered near the plane seemed like flies in comparison.

Through the high-powered binoculars, Philip Stevens was able to get a very close view of the rescue. He saw five of the black-suited frogmen climb onto the wing and

196

move toward the emergency door as it swung open. Water washed up on the wing as the plane rocked in the rough sea. Stevens could see hands passing Eddie out the open door. Eddie was helped by Frank Powers, who Stevens knew to be Martin Wallace's assistant. Powers, and one of the frogmen, carefully helped Eddie down the wing. Next, Mrs. Stern and her daughter, Bonnie, were helped out the door, then down the wing of the plane into the water. One by one the injured were quickly and efficiently removed from the plane and helped to waiting zodiac boats in the water.

As the uninjured guests began to emerge from the plane, the procedure that the teams of frogmen were using became quite clear. One team, stationed on the wing of the 747, helped the passengers out of the emergency-exit door. The passengers were instructed to slide down the wing, which was quite easy for them, since the wing was awash with water. At the edge of the wing, in the water, frogmen caught the passengers as they came off the wing, then helped them swim away from the 747 to waiting zodiac boats. Then, when a zodiac boat was full, it would transport its cargo of rescued passengers back to the *Cayuga*. As each of the zodiacs was unloaded, it would hurry back to the rescue site for more.

Stevens returned his gaze to the emergency exit of the 747. He saw Emily Livingston at the door, and with her was Nicholas St. Downs. She boldly stepped out onto the wing—not even waiting for a frogman to help her. Even amidst this tension and suspense, Philip Stevens had to smile to himself. It was so like Emily. Then the passengers came out of the plane more swiftly, and Stevens was able to pick out the faces of these friends he knew and loved.

Finally he saw the person he had been looking for ever since he took up the binoculars. There, among the guests, with a helpful frogman's arm around her, was his daughter, Lisa. She carried Benjy in her arms. And, as Gallagher had told him, they seemed unharmed. Stevens watched as they slid down the wing and into the water.

Anxiously he looked on as they were both helped into a waiting zodiac boat. Soon they would be on the *Cayuga*, with him.

Philip Stevens took down his binoculars. He found that he couldn't see anything. His eyes were clouded with tears. He realized that for perhaps the first time in his life, he was crying—crying tears of happiness.

Next to Philip Stevens on the bridge, Captain Mackenzie had been intently watching the operation from the beginning. Although he wanted the passengers out of the plane and safely on board the *Cayuga* as much as Philip Stevens did, his concentration was directed more to the details and procedures involved in the rescue operation.

Mackenzie was pleased with what he saw. Lawson had performed well every step of the way. He had stationed the zodiac boats at the correct distance from the 747. When the plane surfaced, the zodiacs weren't so close that they endangered the men, nor were they so far away that time was wasted in getting to the plane after it was on the surface of the water.

The actual evacuation of the plane was going like clockwork, also. He expected that within ten minutes they'd have the entire 747 cleared of passengers.

But then he saw something that he didn't like at all. At the rear of the 747, one of the lifting bags was rubbing on the jagged, torn metal of the tail. He knew that the rubber and nylon fiber of the bags was tough, but the jagged edge of metal was very sharp, and the rubbing was constant. With the rocking motion of the plane in the water, the bag was repeatedly slammed against the sharp metal edge.

Mackenzie knew that the bags held just enough buoyancy to keep the plane from sinking back into the water. If that bag went, the plane would sink like a stone.

19

Gallagher felt exhaustion building. He stood near the emergency exit of the 747, helping the last of the passengers out onto the wing. Finally, only Eve and Buchek were left in the plane. Eve and Buchek stepped onto the wing together, and Gallagher was moving to help them when it happened.

The lifting bag at the rear of the plane suddenly was torn by the piece of jagged metal that it had been rubbing against. There was a roar of escaping air pressure, and the plane almost rolled over on its side before righting itself again. Gallagher was thrown from his feet, along with Buchek. As he slid down the wing toward the water, Gallagher saw Eve falling backward through the emergency exit and into the main lounge of the 747.

Quickly Gallagher hit the stud on his scuba pack. The stud released, and he was able to shrug the scuba tanks off his back. Suddenly lighter, he was able to clamber back onto the wing of the 747, which rocked violently in the water as the air went out of the lifting bag at the tail. Gallagher ran up the wing. He looked over his shoulder for a second and saw a member of the scuba team helping Buchek to a boat. Then, without a moment's hesitation, Gallagher pushed himself through the open emergency exit and entered the main lounge of the 747, desperately hurrying to find Eve.

Once inside the main lounge, Gallagher hurried to Eve, who was lying on the floor, somewhat dazed. Gallagher knelt down and helped her to her feet.

Eve gasped as she looked toward the emergency exit. The floor of the plane was tilting as the tail sank back into the water, and tons of water were pouring back into the plane.

As the water thundered into the emergency exit, Gallagher knew that he had to find another way out of the plane. The plane was subsiding, and the floor was starting to get steeper with each passing second. "The cockpit! Quick!" he said to Eve. Then, taking her hand, he began to run toward the forward part of the main lounge. They weren't fast enough. A wave of water caught them, throwing them to the floor. Choking in the saltwater, Gallagher grabbed Eve's hand again and hauled her to her feet. The two of them began to struggle through the rapidly rising water. Gallagher knew that they had to get to the stairs and up to the flight deck. It was their only hope of escape from the plane.

They struggled up the sloping floor of the main lounge, fighting against the water that pulled at them. Dodging the debris that tumbled past, they finally reached the stairs.

Gallagher pushed Eve ahead of him up the stairs. The angle of the plane was becoming so steep now that Eve had an incredible amount of difficulty as she climbed.

Gallagher followed her up the stairs, the water boiling up around him. The two of them struggled to the top of the stairs, followed by waves of water as the stairs became nearly horizontal. The plane, Gallagher knew, was very close to being totally under water again.

Somehow the two of them made it into the cockpit of the 747. They had to crawl inside and stand on the bulkhead. The nose of the plane pointed skyward, and the plane shook and bucked as it went down into the water, tail-first.

Desperately Gallagher threw the lever on the cockpit's emergency exit. He swung the hatch open, grabbed Eve's hand, and literally pushed her out of the door. Then, without waiting an instant, he jumped after her.

Outside the cockpit, the sea boiled as the 747 continued

plunging down into the water. Gallagher swam toward Eve, and she joined him in swimming as hard as they could away from the sinking plane. Already they felt a strong undertow caused by the aircraft. It was an undertow that, they knew, would grow stronger and was capable of pulling them down with the 747.

Overhead, there was the beating roar of an SH-3 helicopter. The copter pilot had seen Eve and Gallagher in the water and was now hovering overhead. Quickly the copter crew lowered the rope ladder, and Gallagher reached for it, missing it narrowly. The copter hovered closer, and Gallagher reached for the ladder again. This time he was able to grab it. As the copter reduced its altitude somewhat, Gallagher was able to get one leg and one arm through the rungs of the latter. With his other arm he grabbed Eve Clayton and held her tightly to him. Then the helicopter began to pull up, hoisting them out of the water and away from the nose of the 747, which disappeared in a whirlpool of raging water and debris.

The copter hovered in place, and the crew members reeled in the rope ladder. Finally they had reeled enough of the ladder in to help Eve and Gallagher into the copter.

Philip Stevens and Captain Mackenzie had watched breathlessly as the lifting bag ruptured and collapsed. The tail of the plane began to sink immediately. They watched through their binoculars and saw Eve disappear inside the plane, then Gallagher go in after her. Stevens watched in shock and total horror as the big plane began filling with seawater. Then, minutes later, he had seen them climb out of the cockpit hatchway, drop into the water, and be picked up by one of the hovering helicopters.

He held his binoculars on the 747 until the nose of the plane vanished beneath the waves for the last time.

Then he watched as the last of the zodiacs skipped over the waves of the ocean, bringing the remaining passengers back to the *Cayuga*. He knew that they must be cold, wet, tired, and in shock. But they were alive! He turned to Captain Mackenzie. His voice cracked with emotion.

"Captain, I don't know how to thank you enough. I'll never be able to repay you."

Captain Mackenzie smiled. "I think we owe our thanks to those scuba teams, Mr. Stevens.

Stevens shook Mackenzie's hand, then handed his binoculars to one of the sailors on the bridge. Down on the quarterdeck, the last of the rescued passengers were being brought up the gangway. The entire quarterdeck was in an immense confusion as swarms of medical personnel, frogmen, and wet and shivering friends of Philip Stevens met and laughed and hugged each other in gratitude for the success of the rescue. Stevens wanted to be among them. But most of all he wanted to see for himself that his daughter and grandson were safe. Excusing himself, Stevens left the bridge and started down the stairs toward the quarterdeck.

He climbed down the stairs swiftly, for he knew that somewhere down there were Lisa and Benjy, as well as people he had known and been close to for many years of his long life.

An ensign took his arm and helped him as he stepped onto the slippery deck. He thanked the man and started to make his way through the chaos, the jubilation, and the sheer energy that remained after the rescue operation. Three divers, still in wet suits, jostled him as they hurried below deck.

Then, at the far end of the deck, he saw Lisa and Benjy. He knew then that his daughter and his grandson were the two most precious things in his life. He ran through the jostling crowd to them. Lisa opened her arms, and they embraced.

"Oh, Dad," he heard her say, "I love you."

They were words he would have given his entire fortune to hear, words that healed the terrible wounds they had shared between them for so long. He kissed and hugged her to him. Then Lisa leaned down and picked Benjy up and held him. Stevens looked at the boy and thought that he bore a distinct resemblance to himself. But, Philip Stevens wistfully conceded, that was probably what all grandfathers thought about their grandchildren.

"Hello, Benjy," he said. "I'm your grandpa."

Benjy just giggled.

A radioman approached the happy group. He carried a radio message in his hand. He showed the message to Stevens.

"Excuse me, Mr. Stevens, but do you know this man?"

Stevens looked at the note and broke into a smile. "I certainly do," he said. "I think I'll deliver this message personally, thank you." Stevens turned and gave Lisa and Benjy another hug. "I'll be right back," he said. Then he began threading his way through the members of the crew and the rescued passengers, looking for someone.

He couldn't spot the man he was looking for, but he saw his old friend Nicholas St. Downs, and with him was Emily Livingston. They were holding tightly to each other, soaked to the bone. He smiled and waved toward them, then hurried on his way. He saw Dr. Herb Williams, and then was approached by Julie Denton. There was a look of great concern and worry on the young girl's face.

"Mr. Stevens," she said, crying, "where's Eve? I can't find her."

"She's all right, Julie." Stevens warmly took her hand. "Don't worry. She's been rescued."

"And Captain Gallagher?"

"Him too."

Stevens spotted Frank Powers. Martin Wallace was not with him, and that was unusual. "Excuse me," he said to Julie. He walked over to Frank Powers.

"Where's Martin?" he asked.

Frank looked at Philip Stevens. Immediately Stevens knew, from Frank's expression, that Wallace had not survived.

"He didn't make it, sir. He died trying to rescue us. When Captain Gallagher got out of the plane."

"And Karen?" Stevens asked.

Powers just shook his head.

"I'm deeply sorry," Stevens said.

Powers shook his head in agreement, then moved away.

At the other end of the quarterdeck, Stevens finally saw Eddie, lying on a stretcher, where a medic was looking at his injured leg. Stevens hurried toward him. "How are you feeling, Eddie?" Stevens said.

Eddie looked pale, but his spirits were high. "I feel pretty good, Mr. Stevens," he said, "considering."

Stevens smiled. "I think you'll feel much better when you read this," he said. He handed the radio message to Eddie.

As Eddie read the message, his face lit up instantly. "Hey," he shouted, "will you look at this! This is wonderful." Then he read aloud from the message. "'Mother doing well. Twin girls. Seven pounds each.' Will you believe that, I'm a father! This is great!"

Philip Stevens smiled. As a father himself, he knew all the joys and sorrows that being a parent brought.

"It is great, Eddie. It's a lot of things."

Philip Stevens stood up as the two corpsmen lifted the stretcher. They stood for a moment as Eddie shook Stevens' hand. "Thanks for the news," he said.

Stevens warmly shook his hand. Then Eddie was carried off. As his gaze followed Eddie, Philip Stevens saw Chambers, the co-pilot. His wrists manacled, Chambers was being led to confinement by two sailors. Anger boiled up in Stevens. He knew that the law would deal with Chambers, but what penalty was sufficient for a crime as horrible as the one Chambers had committed?

Stevens turned. He saw Buchek at the ship's railing, his arm in a sling. Buchek was gazing off over the sea toward the spot where the aircraft had gone down. Stevens remembered the long hours that he and Buchek had spent together in the preliminary planning of the airplane. They had come to like and respect each other. It was strange. He and Buchek had been together on the 747 project really since even before the beginning. And now they were together at the end. He moved toward Buchek. Buchek turned. He gave a weak smile. He was glad to see Stevens, but his thoughts were still with the tragedy that had befallen them.

"Hi, Phil."

"How's the arm?"

Buchek moved it slightly, as if to show that there was no real damage. "It's okay," he said. "I guess." He turned and looked out over the ocean again. There were storm clouds approaching in the east, and it gave the sky a melancholy cast.

"You know, Phil," Buchek said, "I keep thinking about the ones who didn't make it." It almost sounded as though Buchek were blaming himself.

"You did the best you could," Stevens told him. "That's all that anybody could ask."

Buchek took a deep breath. "I suppose you're right." Then he looked at Philip Stevens. His brow wrinkled with the emotion that he felt. He smiled to himself. "You know, Phil..." Then he was silent.

"What?"

"Sometimes... sometimes just being alive is about the best thing there is."

Philip Stevens smiled. He leaned against the railing. There was so much to Buchek's words. "I know," he said.

The helicopter crew had given Gallagher and Eve a large blanket. Now the two of them sat on the floor of the copter, wrapped in the blanket, drying out. As the copter made its way back to the *Cayuga* they held each other close.

Eve shivered, and Gallagher put his arm around her. "Cold?" he asked.

She moved closer to him. "I'm starting to warm up."

Gallagher smiled. "You've got a date with me tonight. In Palm Beach. Remember?"

"How about for the rest of our lives?" she asked.

Gallagher thought about it for a second. "Convince me," he said.

Smiling, she melted into his arms for a long embrace.